STAR-CROSSED

Liz Mallory has always lived in the shadow of her glamorous sister, Harper. The smart "good" girl, Liz became a librarian in their small hometown while Harper left everything—including Liz—behind to conquer the art world in New York. Now, years later, tragedy reunites these estranged women. Reaching out to her sister, Liz finds herself moving into Harper's exclusive estate to care for her troubled nephew, Nick.

This act of kindness, however, becomes much more complicated than Liz ever expected, for she meets the love of her life— a handsome amateur astronomer named David Fields. Under the dome of the observatory David calls home, Liz tastes a passion as deep and vast as the velvety night sky. But David is a man with painful secrets that could eclipse this newfound love—secrets to which Harper holds the key. Can Liz get beyond her own past hurts and reach the stars with David? Does she dare to try? Heaven only knows . . .

"Grayson has a gift for capturing how relationships begin and develop and a sympathetically attuned insight into human nature."

Publishers Weekly

Also by Emily Grayson

THE GAZEBO

The Observatory

a novel

Emily Grayson

HarperTorch
An Imprint of HarperCollinsPublishers

This is a work of fiction. Names, characters, places, and incidents are products of the author's imagination or are used fictitiously and are not to be construed as real. Any resemblance to actual events, locales, organizations, or persons, living or dead, is entirely coincidental.

HARPERTORCH
An Imprint of HarperCollins*Publishers*
10 East 53rd Street
New York, New York 10022-5299

First HarperTorch paperback printing: March 2001
First Morrow hardcover printing: April 2000

HarperCollins®, HarperTorch™, and ❦™ are trademarks of Harper Collins Publishers Inc.

Printed in the United States of America

Visit HarperTorch on the World Wide Web at http://www.harper collins.com

10 9 8 7 6 5 4 3 2 1

TO E. AND B.,
for providing the wonderful, quiet place
in which many
of these pages were written

Chapter
One

∞ Even though my sister and I are twins, throughout our lives no one ever had trouble telling us apart. We weren't identical in any way. It wasn't just the lengths of our hair, or the clothes we wore, although that was part of it. Over the years she let her dark red hair grow long and wild, while I kept mine cut bluntly just above the shoulders. She preferred flowing fabrics, and beads at the throat and wrist, while I usually wore a single antique silver necklace that my mother gave me before she died.

But there was something else about us that people saw: the way that Harper had become the kind of woman who men instantaneously responded to. Unlike Harper, though, I was often overlooked by men. I'd had relationships occasionally, but I never got the sense that any man would feel about me the way most men felt about my sister. I pretended that it didn't really matter, but it did. It would come at me in the middle of the night, when I'd wake up from a dream in which I'd been lying in the arms of some unknown man. The dream would fall away, and I'd be left lying in my bed for the rest of the night, awake and alone.

Then one afternoon, in the middle of a cold, terrible winter, out on a narrow strip of land, I met a man named David Fields. He looked at me for a long time, and for the next few months at least, he never stopped looking. For a while there, he made me feel, I think, the way men often made Harper feel.

Not that I ever knew exactly what my sister felt about anything. As girls, she and I were never close; as adults our coolness toward each other eventually froze over completely, for no particular reason. There hadn't been a falling-out of some kind; it was just that we'd gone through so many awkward years of not liking each other, and now we were fully grown and on our own, and we understood that we didn't need to force a relationship anymore. One day I realized that I couldn't remember the last time I'd talked to Harper, and that I didn't miss her at all.

And then, suddenly, she was back.

Harper returned to my life the day after New Year's Day. It was snowing, and I'd just come home from the Water Mill, a local bar where I'd been with my friends from the Longwood Falls Library, where I was head librarian. It was only the second day of the new year, and already it was shaping up a lot like the old year. Those of us at the library who didn't have spouses or kids at home had gathered at one of the back tables. We were glad to have a chance to just be together and unwind, and equally glad to be away from our silent, wintry houses for just a while longer. I was still feeling warmed from a glass of red wine, and my fingers were salty from a bowl of cashews that had been refilled several times. Now I was sitting alone in my bedroom as I did most nights, getting changed into an old pink nightgown, the news of the world droning dully in the background, when my doorbell rang.

The sound was startling. It was rare for anyone to show up at the house unannounced at night, and so I slipped on a robe, quickly belted it, and headed downstairs. Through the oblong yellow and green panes of stained glass on the front door, I could make out my elderly aunt Leatrice standing on the porch. I opened the door and saw that my aunt was crying. She hurried through the doorway, putting her arms around me, snow in her hair.

"Aunt Leatrice," I said, alarmed. "What is it?"

My beloved aunt—my late mother's sister, a small, birdlike woman of seventy who lived several streets away—stepped back and regarded me. "Oh, Liz," she said, her voice choked and unfamiliar, "something has happened."

She pulled away, shaking her head, and I followed her into the den. My aunt sat in one of the green wing chairs that faced the fire, and I perched nervously on the edge of the other, waiting for her to collect herself enough to be able to continue. I was afraid she was going to say that something had happened to Harper. Immediately, I could see my sister in a high-speed car accident on a superhighway, or in the crash of a private plane somewhere in Europe. I took a breath and steeled myself for the news; it would be strange and terrible, but I wasn't sure I would cry.

Instead, what my aunt said was, "It's Doe."

Doe: my niece. My sister's daughter. Eight years old. A redhead.

"There was a sledding accident," my aunt went on. "It happened this morning, in Stone Point. She was going down a hill. They don't understand it; this was a place where children go sledding all the time. But something happened, a chunk of ice in the path, and the sled caught, and there was a tree, and she was killed."

"Oh my God," I heard myself say.

My aunt began crying again. I helped her out of her damp coat, poured her some brandy in one of the large snifters my father used to drink from, and built a small, clumsy fire in the hearth. The fire popped and whistled while my aunt continued to sob and drink. Eventually, the fire died down and my aunt, too tired to keep crying, fell asleep in the chair, her head fallen back, mouth open, snoring a little in the way that elderly people often do. The brandy snifter, now empty, dropped from her hand and rolled onto the carpet, not breaking. I picked up the glass, covered my aunt with an afghan blanket I'd knitted one winter when I'd been bored and had plenty of time on my hands. Then I shut off the lights, poked at the ashes in the fireplace one last time, and went upstairs to bed.

The fact was, I didn't know Doe. I'd seen

her once, a week after she was born, at a party her mother threw at the Stone Point house. Stone Point is a wealthy town on the Long Island Sound. All the houses there are huge and look out over the water and have names; my sister's house is called The Eaves. Stone Point is an old town with a history; presidents have vacationed there, and a famous yacht race takes place there every August, and once, back in the 1960s, a beautiful female Olympic swimmer named Maggie Thorpe dove into the water off the Point and was never seen again. My sister's town is a place of glamour and genteel drama, and the one time I'd visited there for her baby's welcoming party, I'd left feeling more inadequate than ever.

That day, the rooms on the first floor of Harper's house had been crowded with guests drinking champagne from long flutes and nibbling smoked salmon on toast points. Everyone was talking and laughing and arguing loudly about topics I knew nothing about, such as ice fishing and the restorative mud baths of Italy. Extravagant baby gifts were presented: a stuffed bear as big as a refrigerator, a child-size Fiat with a real engine and leather bucket seats. Lively rock music was playing over the speakers that hung from the upper corners of every room.

At one point, my sister's newborn Domenica—who'd been instantly nicknamed Doe—was produced from a distant room upstairs, held aloft by a nurse, a proud Irishwoman in a white uniform, and for a moment the deafening noise of the party softened. I remember staring into the eyes of that little baby who had a sprig of red hair that was the same color as Harper's and mine. Something caught in my throat in that moment, but after the applause and the exclamations, the nurse and baby vanished again, and the guests were free to resume their drinking and shouting.

I briefly considered retrieving the gift I'd placed on a table in the foyer when I arrived—a simple baby doll in a red-checked outfit—and sending something more extravagant later. But in the end I hesitantly left it there, and a week later I received a cordial but impersonal thank-you note from my sister and her husband, Carlo Brico, a much older Italian businessman and art collector. I didn't know Carlo at all, and hadn't even been invited to their wedding, which was described in the paper as "intimate," and had apparently taken place on a barge on a canal in Venice. When, a year after Doe's birth, an invitation arrived for a party in honor of the birth of Harper's second child, a boy named Nick, I declined.

My aunt Leatrice, however, was involved in all their lives, and she kept me aware of the children's progress over the years: how Doe loved horses and ballet class and ice cream, and was as idiosyncratic as her mother; how Nick was the serious one, quiet and intelligent like Carlo but sometimes moody and unresponsive. From time to time my aunt even mentioned details of my sister's life that she felt I should know, and I assume that when she spoke to Harper, she did the same about me. Though really, it's not as though there was much to tell in my case; life as the head librarian in a small-town library isn't exactly something that would have captivated my sister.

It was Aunt Leatrice who studiously wrote letters to Harper, made phone calls, and requested school photographs of her grand-niece and grandnephew, which she then religiously pasted in a photo album and showed to me. Every time I looked at pictures of those children I saw what I was missing, but there was nothing to do about it. It was Aunt Leatrice—not me—who had somehow stayed in my sister's good graces, and who got to know the children over the years and loved them deeply. All of which made me wonder now, as I rested my head back against the pillow on my bed and closed my eyes, why exactly I was crying.

When the sun came up in the morning I felt so heavy-hearted that it was difficult to get out of bed and start my day. Once upon a time I'd lived in this room with Harper, though we'd barely spent any time in it together except to sleep. Now the place no longer bore a resemblance to that girlhood room. The striped rose wallpaper was gone, and so were the twin beds with their nubbly chenille spreads. When I moved back into the house after my parents' deaths, I hadn't wanted to sleep in their bedroom; it seemed somehow just wrong. That room I turned into a big, wonderful office, with an old roll-top desk and plenty of books everywhere. The room Harper and I had shared remained mine, though now completely redecorated with a big brass bed and blond wood furniture.

The house had long ago been rid of its traces of my sister, except for one. Inside the pantry off the kitchen were the old pencil markings on the door that my mother had drawn to measure our heights over time. Always, we were head to head, Harper and I, twin sisters who were nothing alike in the ways that matter.

From the beginning we were known as "the Mallory Girls." Or, sometimes, "*those* Mallory girls." Longwood Falls, where we lived from the day we were born, is a small town in upstate New York. It's the sort of place where everyone knows everyone's business, and where people often took it upon themselves to discuss that business. "Liz Mallory is so quiet," I'd been told they would say. "So responsible and courteous." Then, looking furtively around, they would add, "But, now, her *sister*, she's a real original. Not to mention a wildcat."

And it was true. Harper was wild, but she was also accomplished. She did everything first, before anyone else had thought of doing it. She dressed with her own self-invented style and elegance, and she attracted every male within shouting distance. She created collages out of scraps of material, machine parts, and discarded household items—things it would never have occurred to me could be used in that way. She was an artist and a rebel, and she was both infuriating and formidable. But wherever she went, people knew she was there.

Harper never confided in me, never asked me how I was doing, how I was feeling, whether I wanted to come join her and her pack of friends who seemed more sophisticated than my slightly shy, hesitant crowd. She would ride down Bridge Street in Warren Jett's vintage convertible, drinking from a bottle of tequila, her head thrown back, hair blowing, singing old Beatles songs.

By the time high school ended, she'd been in love several times already—each relationship complete with endless phone conversations, arguments, and dramatic breakups. When we graduated, it was clear what our futures would be; everyone knew that Harper was headed for New York City, where she was going to attend art school and become a famous painter, while I was certain to stay right here and have a more average, uneventful life.

Which isn't to say that I was a complete wallflower. Occasionally, boys were interested in me, and later on, men, and I became involved with a few of them over the years, but it was always hard for me to thoroughly enjoy myself, or to imagine that any of these relationships might last. A couple of the ones I'd gone out with had already dated Harper and been dumped by her. I was an afterthought, the sensible alternative to my exciting but maddening sister. And even when I went out with someone she hadn't already been involved with, he always wanted to know all about her. She was the center of everyone's attention, not me. So, in a sort of defensive stance, I never allowed myself to get too close to any man, too intimate, because I feared he'd be disappointed by what he found. And I never really experienced pleasure.

Pleasure was for other people, I assumed. Pleasure was for Harper. And she did experience a great deal of pleasure, at least from the little I glimpsed of her. Mostly, as the years passed and she went from a young, white-hot prodigy in the art world boom years of the 1980s to a figure of lasting prominence, I heard about her goings-on from my proud but bewildered parents. After they died, I heard about her from Aunt Leatrice, and from reading about Harper in the tabloids, which I would buy at the tobacco shop downtown. There she would be in some gossip column: "Who was the dark-haired man in Armani sharing a plate of mahimahi with painter HARPER MALLORY at the Ozone Club last night?" Or else I would see an announcement of one of her art shows in the *New York Times.* "Harper Mallory: Recent Works" it would say, though I was never invited to the openings.

She was rich and famous, and I had a modest life on a small scale, like most people. My job as head librarian at the Longwood Falls Library gave me a great deal of responsibility, and I took pride in what I did. Libraries were, of course, fully automated by now, and had been plagued by cutbacks, but there was still a lot of work to be done planning various programs. But sometimes, as I walked through all that wooded silence, I just wanted to scream. Where was *my* chance at something wonderful? Where was *my* dark-haired man, *my* big career, *my* beautiful children? Where was *my* life?

After my parents died within a year of each other—my mother first, of a long struggle with cancer, then my grieving father of an unexpected heart attack—I made the decision to move back into the white frame house where I'd grown up. Harper didn't care; her lawyers weren't concerned with the money that might be generated from the potential sale of the house. One of her paintings, those large canvases with the haunted, slightly surreal faces of men and women on them, would have fetched as big a price as the house would have. We saw each other briefly at our parents' funerals; after the reception and some awkward moments of forced conversation, she was gone in the shiny black Town Car that had brought her.

∞

That was over a decade earlier. Now my sister and I were thirty-six. Harper had settled into a life of wealth and fame that would be hers forever. Three years ago, my sister's marriage ended, and Carlo, a distracted, older man without much time to give his children, had moved back to Milan, where he remarried and had a baby with his new wife. Time passed; Nick turned seven, and Doe turned eight. It was said by my aunt that Doe was Harper's favorite, because she reminded her of herself.

On the morning after my niece was killed, I nervously picked up the telephone and dialed the house in Stone Point. The phone number was written in my address book, though I had never once called it. After so many years, it would have been difficult to imagine what to say to Harper under any circumstances; under these circumstances, it was impossible, so I didn't even try. Instead, I found myself listening to the phone ring and ring, and thinking about the echo it must be making inside that house—that mansion, really, with its tumble of rooms and picture windows looking out toward the Long Island Sound, where the fog swirled and Connecticut was a vague mirage in the middle distance. Finally a man answered.

"Mallory residence," he said quietly. "How may I help you?" My sister had never changed her name when she married Carlo. She'd already become famous by then under the name Harper Mallory, and even if she hadn't, I couldn't really see her parting with such a crucial piece of her identity.

"I'd like to speak to Ms. Mallory," I said.

"I'm sorry," the man went on. "She's not speaking to anyone."

"This is her sister," I tried.

But that didn't move him. "As I said, she's not speaking to anyone," he said, his voice slightly firmer now, the way he'd obviously been trained when he came to work for Harper.

"I need to know about the funeral," I stammered. "I'm going to come, of course." I paused, then added, rather absurdly, "I'd like to help her. If there's anything I can do . . ."

There was an uncomfortable silence, and then the man said, "The funeral is to be to-morrow. The Old Stone Point Church at noon."

"Thank you," I said. Then, impulsively, I added, "Is she all right?" I knew it was a ridiculous question. How could my sister possibly be all right? The servant didn't even try to answer, but bypassed the question entirely.

"At noon, then," he repeated, and then he quietly said good-bye.

The roads were bad throughout the entire six-hour trip to Stone Point, and even with the snow tires on I had to drive very slowly, the wipers whooshing as they kept the front window clear of slushy rain. Aunt Leatrice sat beside me, but neither of us could bear to talk very much. When we arrived in Stone

Point, the pretty church was as crowded as I'd expected, but even though there were a few art-world celebrities present, no clusters of people leaned together, and no cell phones chirped. The circumstances were much too terrible for any of that, much too sad.

I looked around the church for Harper, but didn't see her anywhere. Maybe she was among the group of women up front in those picture-frame black hats that obscured their faces, or maybe she was somewhere off in the wings, too upset to appear in public. In any event, I had no time to find her, for the service started soon after I arrived, and my aunt and I had to quickly find seats in the back.

Suddenly, a man stood as I looked around for a place to sit, and he gestured for me and Aunt Leatrice to take his place. We didn't exchange words, so I can't say we actually met at that moment. I only took in the fact that he was a handsome man, freshly shaven, who looked a little uncomfortable in a suit. His name, though I didn't know it at the time, was David Fields. He was the man I would soon fall in love with, but, of course, I didn't know this either. It's strange the way that happens: how you can come upon someone and have no idea that this person who means nothing to you will someday mean everything.

I helped Aunt Leatrice sit down and then I squeezed in beside her, nodding thanks to the man who had given us his seat, and then turning away from him. The church, a small, crumbling stone building, was inadequately heated, and I found myself shivering. When the coffin was carried in—tiny and simple, made of a polished rosewood that was almost the color of Doe's hair, and her mother's— the entire congregation seemed to slump down and cry in unison. Their tears contin- ued throughout the psalm recited by the minister, and during the eulogies given by people who included Doe's teacher at the

Craighead School, a young, stunned-look-ing woman, and Doe's best friend, a little girl named Caitlin.

Caitlin, who at age eight was blonde and flushed with nervousness, stood up in front of everyone, clutching a doll to her chest. "See this doll?" said Caitlin into the micro-phone, her voice a trembling, hoarse whis-per. "Doe gave it to me."

I looked at the doll; it was faded and old, and wore a tattered red-checked outfit. Something about the doll seemed familiar, and after a moment a chill traveled through me as I realized this was the doll that I had given my niece when she was born.

"She said it was for being her best friend," Caitlin continued. "It was *her* doll since she was born, but she wanted me to have it." She paused, looking sidelong toward the coffin, then away again, then back. "I'll al-ways keep this doll, Doe," she said. "And I promise to take care of her forever."

My aunt was leaning against me. I leaned back. If I, who hadn't known my niece at all, was feeling this distraught, I couldn't even imagine what Harper must be going through. At the end of the service, when everyone stood, I once again looked for my sister, but still I couldn't find her. I figured I'd soon see her back at the house, where the reception was to be held, and so I started to head out the open double doors, shepherding my aunt along beside me.

As I was about to leave, though, something caught my eye. It was the back of a woman's head, the red hair carelessly hacked off as short as a boy's, as though it had been done in a great hurry, with blunt shears. Something about the slope of the shoulders and the long neck looked familiar, and my first thought was that this was one of my relatives, perhaps a distant cousin who had flown in from somewhere far away. I remembered that there were a few Mallory cousins in Des Moines, Iowa. Just then, the woman turned her head and met my gaze. We looked at each other for a moment, and then I knew.

It was my sister, and she had cut off all her hair. This utterly changed person who stood facing me in the cold winter church was practically a stranger to me, a stranger with a bad haircut and eyes that appeared as lifeless and frozen as the trees along the road I'd been traveling for hours.

They say that twins always retain some memory of the time when they were two swimmers enclosed in a warm, silent place, and that even when those twins grow up and live entirely separate lives, if something terrible happens to one twin, the other can't help but be changed, too. Harper had experienced something unbearable, and I suddenly had a glimpse of the extent of it. She seemed to have disappeared from the world, had swum away forever and been replaced by someone strange and different. And the thing was, I felt strange and different, too. It was as though she and I were locked together now, and the intensity of it made me feel panicky, overwhelmed. Though she let herself be kissed by me, let herself be stiffly embraced, and politely accepted the inadequate words of sorrow that I had to offer, I knew enough to be frightened.

Chapter
Two

∞ The house was filled with whispers. At the reception throughout that first long day, guests stood in clusters and talked in low voices. They were whispering because Harper was nearby and they didn't want to say anything that would possibly upset her any further. But whenever I glanced at my sister from across her huge living room, I saw that she was beyond the reach of their voices: in fact, she was drunk.

The last time I'd seen her drunk like this was in high school, when she'd come home at 3 A.M. after a night of partying with her friends. I remember waking up to hear her moving around downstairs, the suction sound of the refrigerator being opened and closed, and then a few small collisions with

furniture. She accidentally knocked against
a small end table in the living room, shaking
all the little Steuben glass figurines on it that
my mother collected, letting them clang
against one another like wind chimes, yet
not breaking even one. Later, Harper came
upstairs and entered our bedroom, bringing
with her the scent of bourbon tempered by
the frangipani perfume she wore back then.
She fell asleep lying on her back and fully
dressed, and as I looked over at her I saw the
way her long hair flowed across the pillow,
and how beautiful her face was, even
though she was drunk.

Now, practically a lifetime later, her beauty
was in hiding, and she sat on the long white
couch of her living room, a fragile, drunken
woman with shorn-off hair. In her hand was a
glass of bourbon that had been refilled many
times by a butler who didn't dare try to dis-
suade her each time she demanded a refill.
No one sat with her, and if anyone came near,
she turned away. It was clear that she didn't
want to be touched or talked to. When I

glanced over at the couch again, I saw that she had put the glass down on the coffee table and was leaving the room.

As I watched her go, I felt the pressure of a cool hand on my shoulder, and I looked up to see my sister's ex-husband, Carlo. He was a banker, twenty years older than me, with a large, handsome face and enormous hands. He spoke five languages, and knew how to get his way in all of them. His dark hair was raked back off his face with some sort of expensive Italian gel, and he wore a tapered, dark, double-breasted suit that must have cost millions of lire at some hushed men's boutique on a boulevard in Milan. Carlo had been traveling with his new wife and infant son in the Pyrenees when Doe was killed, and had been unreachable that first day. Because of this, he'd arrived from Europe this morning, just in time for her funeral. He was a remote man who, since the divorce, had seen Nick and Doe just once a year, but it was clear that he was terribly broken by the death.

"Carlo," I said, standing and lightly taking the hand of my ex-brother-in-law, whom I'd met only a couple of times. At first I was surprised that he even knew who I was after all this time, but then I remembered that he *had* to remember, for I bore a resemblance to his ex-wife. "I don't know what to say," I began lamely. "I'm very sorry."

He waved away my words. "I have been a not so good father," he said in a halting voice, heavy with accent. "I almost feel that I have no right here at The Eaves. Your sister, Harper, she hates me. Our divorce was not pleasant, to say the least." He gave a small, bitter laugh. "And now my Doe is gone," he went on, "and Harper will not speak to me." He paused, shaking his head slowly, wiping his eyes with a linen handkerchief. "They tell me she will not speak to anyone," he said. "No more than a few words. She has closed herself up completely."

"I can see that," I said.

"It is not good for her," he said. "She must

talk to people, she must cry with them, or else she will not be able to cope." Suddenly, Carlo's eyes brightened briefly. "Perhaps," he said, "she will talk to you."

"Me? I doubt it," I told him. "She's never had too much to say to me before. I can't imagine why she'd suddenly start now."

"You are her closest blood relative," Carlo said. "That counts for something, I think. I know that she is difficult. Everyone who has ever met her knows that," he said. "But please, if you would at least try, I'd be very grateful, Liz."

Liz. I was startled. There was something about this handsome, urbane man addressing me by name that made me feel peculiar, reminding me of how long it had been since a man had said my name in an urgent voice. How long it had been since I'd had a lover. Harper's life had been populated with them; handsome men had seemed to appear whenever she was around, both before and after her marriage. She had treated love lightly; at least it seemed that way to me.

Now I was embarrassed by my sudden surge of feeling at this inappropriate moment; all it had taken was an attractive man saying my name aloud with a certain kind of intensity. I flushed with shame at my reaction, and it reminded me that it wasn't only Harper who had closed herself off.

I looked at Carlo. In a day or two he would say good-bye to his ex-wife and son and be back on a private jet to his new family in Milan. I couldn't understand how he could leave so quickly, but there were plenty of things about the geometry of other people's lives that I didn't understand. Without really knowing why, I nodded and told Carlo I would at least try to talk to Harper, but that he shouldn't expect much.

Walking up the wide marble staircase that my sister had recently ascended, I felt like the stand-in for a movie star, following in her path. What would I say to Harper? We'd already had our brief moment together in the church. To try to take it any further would be awkward, I knew, but still I continued walking up the stairs, because I'd told Carlo I would do this.

There were many rooms in the lushly carpeted second-floor hallway; through open doors I could see antique clocks and mirrors and, in one room, a small bronze Degas statue of a dancing girl. I noticed that a door was shut, and this one I immediately knew to be Harper's. I knocked hard, and there was no reply, so I knocked again. Still no reply. Now I turned the large crystal knob and entered the room. It was unlit, but the natural light from the windows threw a bluish spill over everything.

My sister was lying there on her back, fully dressed with her eyes closed, the same way she had done that night she had come home drunk in high school.

I stood right beside her and said her name aloud. After a moment, she opened her eyes and said, "Go away, Liz." Then she closed her eyes again.

"I don't want to go away," I told her. "Aunt Leatrice and I drove all the way here. And it wasn't for the hors d'oeuvres," I tried.

"Well, if it was for the conversation," she said, "then I have to disappoint you. I'm not in a talkative mood."

"Please, Harper," was all I could say, though I wasn't even sure what I meant by that.

"Please *what*?" My sister's voice was dry, sour, unrecognizable. "You'll have to excuse me if I don't rise to the occasion. I'm not exactly in the mood to meet my social obligations." Her voice was growing rawer and angrier by the word. "Thank you for coming all this way, Liz. Thank Aunt Leatrice. Thank anybody downstairs who's drinking my liquor and eating my food and talking about the latest opening and trying to meet the right gallery owner and already moving on with their lives. They can all get along quite well without me." She paused, then she added, "And they will."

Her words were strange, disturbing, and seemed to hint of hurting herself. "What do you mean?" I asked nervously.

She opened her eyes again and gave me a questioning look. Then she understood. "I don't mean *that*," she said, and her voice softened. "Not that I haven't thought about it, believe me. But I couldn't do that to Nick. I have to find a way to survive." She waited a moment, then said, "I mean I'm going away for a while. I have a house on an island off the Florida coast. It's very remote. Sometimes I go there to work. But now, I think I should go there and just . . . completely disappear for a while. I'm going out of my mind, Liz. I don't know what else to do."

"Are you sure it's a good idea to be all alone?" I asked.

"No," she said tightly. "I'm not. But do you have any better suggestions?"

I shook my head. Harper was right; I knew

∞

nothing about this level of grief. I couldn't even begin to comprehend the magnitude of it. I was quiet, just looking at her, taking in her shorn hair, her face that was blotchy from so much crying and drinking, and her words, which were starting to make sense to me. My twin sister was telling me that she, who had always surrounded herself with so many people, so much activity, had reached a point at which she was desperate for silence.

"Well," I tried, "if you ever need anything—"

"Oh, Liz," she said, and now her voice was barely a whisper. "It's too late for you and me. We've never been friends; we've never even liked each other." She paused. "I can say that, can't I?"

"Yes," I said softly. "You can."

It was true, of course. I walked over to the windows then; I'm not sure why. I stood looking out over the snowy road and the thicket of woods beyond. The Eaves was made up of a great deal of property; no other houses were around, and so I could see no friendly lights from other homes, or the reassuring roll of smoke from other chimneys. The landscape was simply cold and forlorn and slipping into late afternoon half-light.

Suddenly, I was surprised to see a figure moving along the road. I realized that it was a child walking. And then, with a start, I realized that it was my nephew, Nick. *Nick*. He had been forgotten by almost everyone in the middle of all the drama. No one else would have seen him now, for they were all sitting in the living room, where the windows looked out over the Sound, but Nick was walking along the road in front of the house. He was heading away from home, going down the road toward who knew where.

I felt suddenly afraid for him, and the fear took the form of a pressure in my chest that I hadn't experienced before. It was the kind of thing a mother might feel when one of her children wanders off. "There's Nick," I said. "Walking in the snow."

Harper glanced out the windows. "So he is," she said, seeming uninterested.

"Should he be out there all by himself?" I asked. "I don't think a car could see him easily today. And besides, it's freezing."

Harper waved her hand vaguely. "He'll be all right," she said. "He's a boy. They manage."

"He's seven years old," I said.

"He'll come in when he's ready," said Harper. "He always does."

I looked at her sharply, realizing that in her state she could only think of her own loss, and very little else. "And what if he doesn't come in?" I persisted. "And what about while you're in Florida on that island. What about then?"

"Sanibel Island," she said. "Jeannette, the cook, will attend to Nick. She does an excellent job. Besides," she added, "I wouldn't be much use to him here. He'd see me lying in bed and crying all day; it would frighten him."

But I couldn't tolerate the idea of my

nephew being left in the care of the cook,
however kindly and maternal she was.
"Harper," I said firmly, "that won't do. He
needs more than that." The strength of my
own voice surprised me.

Apparently, it surprised Harper, too. She
arched an eyebrow at me. "Why, Liz," she
said, "I've never heard you speak with
such . . . conviction."

I felt my face grow warm. "Harper," I said,
"you've got friends here; can't they help?
And, of course, you've got Carlo, at least for
a little while."

"Carlo couldn't care less," she said.

"That's not true," I replied. "I talked to
him. He's very upset. Anyone can see that."

"He barely knew his own children," she
said in a harsh voice. "What kind of a father
is that?"

I didn't know what to say. Doe and Nick
had been my niece and nephew, yet I barely
knew them either. "I'm going dowstairs
now," I said.

"Fine," said Harper.

I turned and looked at her again. She had sunk back against the pile of brocade pillows, her eyes closing. "Do you need anything?" I asked softly.

"Yes," she said. "Tell the butler to bring me a double bourbon."

"All right," I said, though I had no intention of doing so.

The snow was fierce by the time I stepped outside. The leather boots I'd worn today weren't built for weather like this. Though they were thick and lined with fleece, their tread wasn't substantial, and I slipped in the thick, deep snow that was mixed through with ice. But still I kept crunching along the slippery road, heading in the direction of my nephew. I called his name a few times, but either he didn't hear me or he chose not to.

Where was Nick going? I wondered as the snow flew into my mouth and I felt my eyelashes become speckled with ice. The road turned hard to the right and went up steeply. Still I followed him, hoping my boots could tolerate the incline and not send me sprawling backward. Finally we were both at the top of a hill.

Nick was facing away from me and peering downward; I approached him carefully, the way you would approach a deer. He was a small boy in a gray coat that was way too big for him. He wasn't wearing mittens, I saw, and his fingers looked raw. He wasn't wearing a hat, either, and his hair was practically white with snow. He was seven years old, but in some ways he resembled a tiny old man.

"Nick?" I said again, coming forward and touching him on the shoulder. He flinched and turned quickly; apparently he hadn't known I was following him. He stared at me, startled and suspicious. "It's your aunt Liz," I said in a loud voice, trying to speak over the wind.

He studied me a moment, surprised. Then, apparently seeing my resemblance to his mother, he quickly nodded.

"Let me take you inside," I said.

He shook his head and moved slightly away. Instinctively, I trailed after him, looking in the direction he was looking. I understood that this was the place where Nick's sister had been killed.

I followed his gaze down the steep hill. The snow that had fallen in the last two days had covered over any traces of the accident. Now this was just a plain white hill with trees on either side, the kind of hill sledded down by children everywhere. The kind that Harper and I used to sled down in Longwood Falls. I remember how I would primly sit upright on my sled, clutching the steering mechanism and trying to keep it from going too fast, while Harper would lie flat on her stomach, eyes closed for the entire thrill ride.

Now my eyes burned from the wind and from tears not only for the little girl I hadn't known, but also, selfishly, for the girl *I'd* once been, who'd grown up and led such a limited life. Harper and I had slid down our own hill, gathering momentum and creating two distinct paths. She'd gone off into the world with her big career and children and men, and I'd gone off alone. I looked down at my nephew, Nick, in his oversize coat, and I felt an enormous rush of tenderness.

"It's not your fault," I said after a moment, and I'm not sure why I thought to say this. "The accident, I mean."

He looked at me, shocked, and at first I thought he was offended that I would think he had been having such ideas. But then his expression changed slightly, and I knew that I'd been right about him.

"It *is* my fault!" he said with sudden passion. "It was my idea to go sledding; she wanted to make snow angels instead. I told her snow angels were dumb and boring."

"You couldn't have known," I insisted. "No one can ever know. It's mysterious, the way these things happen. You have to believe me: you aren't responsible."

No one had thought to say such a thing to him; no one had even realized he might feel guilty, that he might harbor this feeling silently, for a long time, until it grew inside of him.

"Did my mom send you out here to get me?" he asked, and I shook my head no.

"No one sent me," I said. "I wanted to come."

"Go away," he said. "I don't want you here. Just go away." His voice was the dictator's pout of an angry child, but there was also such an unimaginable sadness beneath it that I would have let him speak to me that way as long as he needed. I stood for a few moments while he continued to tell me to go away, that no one wanted me here, that I should just go back to wherever it was I had come from.

Finally he was done. We stood and regarded each other, and then, in a deadpan voice, I said, "I don't know, maybe I'm crazy, but I'm beginning to get the feeling that you don't want me here."

Nick looked puzzled, then he said, "Are you trying to be funny?"

I nodded. "Trying. But not succeeding, I guess."

"No," he agreed. "Not succeeding at all." He seemed to take some satisfaction from my failure at humor.

I exhaled hard and watched my own breath be released in a burst of vapor. "Come on," I said again, "let's go in," and this time Nick agreed.

So we walked back to the house together, and though he still wore a dark, brooding expression, some unspoken thing was taking place between us, an odd relationship forming in silence and freezing weather between a little boy and a grown woman who didn't know each other.

Once inside, I sat with Nick at the kitchen table while all around us the serving staff efficiently worked, preparing triangular sandwiches with the crusts removed and arranging them in patterns on silver trays. Nick wolfed down six little cheese triangles without much trouble, and he chased them with a tall glass of milk and a wedge of chocolate cake roughly the size of a shoe.

"When was the last time you ate?" I asked, and he just shrugged. I marveled at the appetite of this boy, something I hadn't had the chance to witness before.

I knew almost nothing about children. A long time ago, when I'd been in a relationship with a lawyer in my town named Jeff Hardesty, I'd briefly imagined marrying him and having children. I had always expected love to be clear, vivid, the *it* I'd always heard about. Whatever I'd had with Jeff wasn't *it*, but it was something, and for a while, we'd both convinced ourselves that it was enough.

But it wasn't. At least not for me, not at that point in my life. Jeff and I disentangled from each other, and after a while he moved north to Buffalo, and that was that. Slowly my twenties slipped into my thirties. Occasionally there were other men, but no *it*. All around me, I saw other people fall in love and have children. I went to wedding showers and then baby showers, sitting among crowds of women while a very pregnant friend sat in the middle of the room opening gifts, holding up tiny pastel outfits and crib mobiles from which six little pandas were suspended.

I'd always wanted a family; when I was little, I'd given weddings for my dolls, and then I'd generously blessed them with children. Doll childbirth was a painless event; my dolls simply went to the hospital and returned with a new bundle in their arms. Did I imagine that such things would happen to *me* so easily? That one day I'd fall in love and the next thing I knew I'd be married, and that soon my husband and I would find ourselves surrounded by children? In truth, I hadn't really thought any of it through; I'd just foolishly imagined that a person's life "fell into place." And then I'd sat back and watched as Harper's life fell into place, not mine.

I glanced over at Nick now, and he put down his cake fork. His face was speckled with crumbs, and there was a white slash of milk above his upper lip. There was an intensity to his eyes, and then he said, "It should have been me."

I stared at him, knowing what he meant but not wanting to believe it. "What should have been you?" I asked.

"On the hill," he said. "My mom wished it was me. Doe was her favorite."

"No one would wish something like that," I said. But actually I had no idea of what went on in my sister's mind. "She loves you, Nick," I continued. "I mean, come on, she's your mother."

"Doe was her *daughter*," he said. "They were exactly alike; that's what everyone said. They looked alike, the same red hair, and people said she was willful, just like my mom."

"Do you think so?" I asked.

"I don't know," said Nick, shrugging. "What's *willful* mean?"

In that moment I was reminded that he

was just a little boy, despite his anger and his intensity and his sadness. He was a little boy sitting at a table drinking milk and eating a piece of cake, an ordinary little boy whose feet barely brushed the floor, and who I had missed out on getting to know.

I imagined Nick wandering outside forever, just trudging along that road for so long that he became lost or forgotten, and disappeared into the snow, his footprints soon covered over. I felt an urgency as I looked at him. He was warm now from the heat of the kitchen. His cheeks had returned to their usual color, and the snow was gone from his hair, which had been toweled dry and combed by a maid.

Back in Longwood Falls, my job waited at the red brick library on the corner of Bancroft Road. They would be expecting me there Monday morning. The janitor would say hello to me as I came in, and so would the young woman who worked the checkout desk. I felt safe in that building, surrounded by books—objects that comforted me almost in the way that people were meant to comfort one another.

Ever since the elderly head librarian had died two years ago, I'd been running the place, doing pretty much everything that needed to be done. I created afterschool programs for children and I conducted a book group that was attended by smart women who had some spare time on their hands. The book group gathered once a month after hours in the lounge area, where we all talked and talked, snacking on the terrific, greasy doughnuts from Beckermann's Sweet Shop.

Everyone who came to the library knew me. They knew they could count on me because I was a good worker, and also because, unlike some people who worked there, I didn't have a husband to go home to, or children. I once casually overheard one of the librarians saying to another, "Oh, Liz Mallory is practically *married* to the library."

∞

She hadn't meant it as an insult, but it had upset me all the same.

They expected me back at the library Monday morning. But I wasn't going to go back yet. I wanted to help my nephew, Nick, to keep him company while his mother disappeared to recuperate on Sanibel Island. Even if he didn't want my help, I would take care of him in a way that no one else would. I knew it was the right thing to do, even though Harper would probably say that Nick would be fine here with Jeannette. But he wouldn't be fine. For the first time ever, it was Harper's turn to retreat from the world, and my turn to enter it.

Chapter Three

∞ Soon we were on our own, Nick and I. As I expected, Harper had tried to insist that I didn't need to stay, but she didn't have the heart for a fight. Apparently, she didn't have the heart for anything now. She seemed barely alive, barely responsive. As she was heading out the front door for the car to take her to the airport and Sanibel Island, she commented that for once she was able to pack light. For the first time, she explained, she wouldn't be taking her art supplies with her.

"I don't have it in me anymore," she said. "It's over."

"You can't know that," I answered.

"Yes I can," she said, and the sudden strength of her voice silenced me. "I've locked up the studio forever," she went on. "There's no point in keeping it open. I can't imagine painting again. I mean, who the hell cares?"

"I do," I tried.

"I don't," she said, and she headed out the door.

I stared after her as she swept into the waiting car, and then I watched Nick, on the steps, as he sat looking at her car slowly disappearing down the drive. A few hours earlier, I'd driven Aunt Leatrice to the train station. It's just you and me now, I thought as I gazed down at the fragile, unmoving figure of a seven-year-old boy. It's just you and me and this great big house.

Nick and I were going to have to get to know each other now almost from scratch. The first thing I learned about him was not to ask questions about how he felt, or who his friends were, or what interested him most at school. His favorite reply was a shrug, and usually I accepted these nonresponses and just moved on. I learned to let

∞

Nick lead me where he wanted to go, which turned out to be playing round after round of Monopoly and Clue. When that became boring, we sometimes strapped on cross-country skis and headed out into the endless expanse of snow. My sister's property extended for miles, and every day Nick and I ventured someplace new. At times we just trudged along the shoreline, where the snow was thin and the waves rough, walking for hours without once saying a word. It didn't take me long to realize that what he enjoyed most—whether playing board games or exploring outdoors—was the silence.

At night, after we'd finished eating whatever excellent dinner the cook Jeannette had prepared, we sat on throw pillows in front of the fire in the so-called family room, and I read to him. Nick wasn't a strong reader himself, but he liked to close his eyes and hear the words said aloud. Sometimes, as I read to him, I wished that he would lean his head against my shoulder, but he never did. I wished he would let me offer him the comfort I knew he needed, but not once did the opportunity arise. The books he preferred were stories of action, not emotion, in which boys found themselves accidental passengers on spaceships or freight trains.

Not that Nick himself had ever seen much of the world. When he was younger and his parents were still together, they would often travel to Europe, but they always left the children in Stone Point with the staff. Even now, it was his mother who was traveling, not Nick; every night, no matter how bad a day she'd had, she called from the house off the Florida coast, and Nick supplied her with the highlights of his day. Then he would hand the phone over to me, and in her painfully flat voice my sister would supply me with the highlights of *her* day— telling me whether she managed to get out of bed before noon, or not.

I was sometimes frightened during these calls, not really knowing how Harper was doing. But I tried not to seem too worried, and I reminded her that grief wasn't something you could rush, and to take as long as she needed. And I meant it; the director of the Longwood Falls Library had been surprised when I had asked for a leave of absence, and he was understandably concerned by the word *indefinite,* but under the circumstances, what could he say? Like all family emergencies, this one was unpredictable.

One day, on a walk together, Nick wordlessly led me down a path into the woods behind the house. I'd finally abandoned the inadequate boots I'd brought with me. Now I was wearing my sister's boots, as well as some of the unused clothes that hung in the closet of the guest room where I was staying; Harper had insisted I take anything of hers that I liked, since we wore the same size. After a while, I saw a clearing on the path ahead, and in the center of it a simple frame building. I'd seen it once before and vaguely assumed that it housed Jeannette and the butler, Tom, but I later learned that the household staff lived in apartments on the top floor of the house.

"What is this place?" I asked Nick.

"My mom's studio," he said as we approached. "She does all her painting here."

So this was it, then: the studio that I'd heard so much about over the years. The door was locked with a bulky padlock, so Nick and I stood and looked through the windows, pressing our faces against the cold leaded glass panes.

It was magnificent, a dream place for any artist to work. I'd seen pictures of the studio's interior before in a design magazine, but even those elegant photographs hadn't done the place justice. Harper had created a perfect world for herself in here, an airy, white room with bleached wood floors, cathedral ceilings, and an abundance of sun that bathed the place in the kind of perfect, lemon-colored light that any artist would covet.

The Observatory
∽

Against one wall was a long, paint-spattered table covered with a smorgasbord of art supplies. There were implements of various types and thicknesses, from long industrial rollers to Japanese brushes made up of a few hairs bound together on a slender stick of bamboo. There were stretched canvases, still pristine and untouched, and large, dented silver cans of turpentine and linseed oil. On another wall was an elaborate stereo system. There was a cot in a corner of the room, neatly made, and a kitchenette where meals could be prepared. I thought that an artist working in this studio would find everything she needed here, and would never want to leave.

But Harper had. She had walked away and vowed never to return. I imagined the studio staying just as I saw it now, a ruin frozen in time, its brushes hardening into unusability, its jars of paints drying up, the surfaces of liquid cracking like scorched earth. As I stood looking in through the studio windows, I suddenly felt that this was the saddest place on earth, but as I was about to turn away, something caught my eye.

It was a large canvas, propped up on an easel in the shadows by the far wall of windows. Even though it was mostly abstract, and even though I could barely see it, I could still tell that it was a half-finished painting of a child. And then, from the flame-colored hair and sly, half-closed eyes, I saw that it was supposed to be Doe. I shielded my eyes with my hand and stood looking hard at this painting of Doe, half-finished, that would never be completed.

"So what do you think of my mom's studio?" Nick asked. "Do you like it?"

I straightened and turned from the window. "Yes," I answered, and I understood that he didn't yet know about his mother's decision.

"I could show you something else," he volunteered. "Do you want to see the Point?"

I was cold and would have liked to have

gone inside, but the offer from Nick was so uncharacteristically forthcoming that I quickly answered, "All right."

Stone Point had been named for a long, smooth piece of land that jutted out into the Sound. I'd heard that lovers often stood out on the Point and kissed, and that various marriage proposals had taken place there. Nick and I trudged through the snow toward the Point. By the time we arrived at our destination the afternoon had dropped away, turning to dusk. Stars had already started to come out, dotting the sky here and there.

As we walked out onto the narrow stretch of land I saw that there was a man standing at the tip. He was facing away from us, fiddling with some sort of contraption he had set up. At first I assumed it was one of those tripods used by land surveyors, but then, as we came closer, I saw that I was wrong. The man had a telescope, and it was tipped up toward the heavens. He was tightening the screws, adjusting the thing, and then peering into it, swinging it lightly to the left and then the right, as though searching for something in particular. When he heard us coming, he turned around, and I found myself facing a man who seemed familiar. He appeared to be studying me, too, as if puzzling out who I was. After a moment, it came to me: he was the man at the funeral who had given me his seat.

He was close to forty, tall and lean, wearing a worn leather aviator jacket. His face was handsome, and his hair was wavy and dark brown.

"Have we met?" he asked.

"No," I said. "But I think we saw each other at the church the other day. You gave my aunt and me a place to sit." He nodded, remembering, and seemed about to introduce himself, but all of a sudden Nick stepped forward.

"Mr. Fields," he said. He reached out to shake hands with the man, as he'd most likely been taught. But the man ignored his hand and gave him a hug instead.

"Hey, Nick," he said softly, pulling back to

take a look at my nephew. "I've been thinking about you a lot, you know. Did you get
my letter?"

"Yes," said Nick, seeming both pleased
and deeply embarrassed at the attention.
"Thanks a lot." He looked over at the telescope. "What are you doing?" he asked,
clearly eager to steer the conversation away
from his family's tragedy.

"Trying out my latest toy," said the man.
His voice was soft and hesitant, but rough-
edged, too. "Want to have a look?"

"Sure," said Nick, and the man lowered
the telescope and helped Nick get a good
view of something through the eyepiece. As
Nick stared up at the heavens, the man casually turned to me.

"I'm David Fields," he said. "Nick's
teacher at the Craighead School."

"Liz Mallory," I said, and I extended my
gloved hand. He shook it with a gloved
hand of his own, soft brown leather that had
been broken in over the years. "I'm his
aunt."

∞

"I figured it was something like that," he said. "You're staying with the family?" he asked, and I nodded.

"I'm staying with Nick," I amended. "His mother went away."

"Oh?" He sounded surprised.

"She has a house on an island off Florida," I said, and David nodded. "She said she needed to be completely alone."

"I guess I can understand that," he said. "But what about Nick? How long will his mother be gone?"

"I don't know," I said. "She doesn't know. However long it takes, I guess." And then I regarded Nick. "But not too long, I hope."

He nodded. We stood quietly for a moment, and then he told me in a low voice that he'd been concerned about Nick, wondering how he was going to get along over school break.

"He's doing pretty well," I said. "We've been spending all our time together, playing games, walking around."

"I'm glad to hear that," said David. "I worry."

There was an uncomfortable pause then; we couldn't say too much about Nick's situation because he was standing right there, but it was clear that both of us genuinely cared about this uncommunicative little boy. I was happy that Nick had such a kind teacher. In my entire experience of grade school, I'd never had a male teacher. There was one man who had taught in Longwood Falls, though I hadn't been in his class. He was a kind of male version of a spinster schoolmarm. His name, I still remembered, was Mr. Rembard, and he wore a green button-down cardigan sweater every day and a small red bow tie, and he always brought a damp tuna fish sandwich with him that he ate at his desk.

But David Fields was obviously very different. I liked him right away, and yet I felt uneasy in his presence. I knew that I didn't look very attractive all bundled up in my

∞

bulky winter coat and thick woolen hat. I probably looked kind of ridiculous, I thought, and this depressed me. For some reason, I wanted to look good for this man; I wanted him to like me. This was a very strange sensation, one I hadn't experienced in a long time. It came upon me out of nowhere, at a time when I had hardly been thinking about men.

"Would you like a look through the telescope?" David asked me, and I nodded.

"What were you looking at up there?" I asked.

"Saturn," he said.

"Really? You can see it from here?"

"Sure," he said. "You need a pretty decent instrument, but this one's not too terrible."

To the naked eye, the sky at dusk seemed to contain only the familiar presence of a half-moon, as well as a few stars and the occasional lights of an airplane passing by. But when David adjusted the telescope for me, I looked through it and saw that one of the stars that had looked ordinary before was now, under extreme magnification, miraculously changed into a planet, complete with a set of hazy rings.

"Look at that," I said quietly. "It's just like in all the pictures I've ever seen. It's beautiful."

"Yes," said David. "It really is." He paused. "A few years ago you couldn't have seen those rings even if you'd looked through this telescope," he said.

"Why not?" I asked.

"Because the earth was passing through what's known as the 'ring plane' of Saturn, and the edges of the rings were facing us, edge on, so they would have been invisible."

"Well, I'm glad to see them now," I said, staring at the shimmering rings of Saturn and the muted colors that swam within the sphere of the planet itself. I stood back from the telescope, letting Saturn return to an ordinary pinpoint. Suddenly, as I watched the sky, something shot across it, leaving a diagonal scratch of light in its wake. David and I both stood and watched it go.

"What was that?" I asked, startled. "A shooting star?"

He nodded. "Yes," he said. "Just burning itself out as it goes; that's what they do. Bits of ice turning to fire, nothing more than that."

"Where is it?" Nick asked, searching the sky.

"Gone," David answered. "That's the thing about shooting stars. By the time somebody else sees one, it's too late for you. But you can always keep looking for another one."

Nick did. While he was staring up at the heavens, I asked David how long he'd been watching the sky.

"Practically always," he said with a shrug. "When I was a boy I used to come out here to the Point and look at things for hours. I didn't have a telescope then, only a pair of good binoculars."

"So what were you looking for?" I asked lightly. "UFOs?"

"No," he said, but he didn't elaborate.

"Is it a secret?" I asked, and when he didn't reply, I said, "I know. A mystery woman."

It was an innocent, silly joke, but suddenly David's mood changed completely. He straightened up, turning slightly away from me. "No," he said. "It wasn't a mystery woman." His voice was suddenly cold, as though I'd said something wrong, though I couldn't imagine what had made him so upset. Then he glanced at his watch and said, "Well, I should get back. Excuse me, Nick."

Nick moved away from the telescope and we watched as David quickly packed it up, closing the tripod and unscrewing the long steel columns from one another, collapsing the entire instrument swiftly and easily, as though it were nothing more complicated than a lawn chair. I wanted to ask what it was I'd said to offend him, but I couldn't find the voice. We stood awkwardly in the wind for a moment more as Nick's teacher tucked the telescope under his arm, and then we headed off in different directions.

* * *

For the rest of the evening I felt agitated and upset. The dinner that the cook prepared was comforting and well made—roast chicken and garlic mashed potatoes—but I didn't enjoy it. Afterward, Nick enticed me into a game of Monopoly, and though I played for a while, I finally begged off. I went upstairs to my bedroom, which was located in a wing used only for guests. I was currently the only guest in the house, and the wing was always as quiet as a museum, or a library. I was reminded for a moment of the library back in Longwood Falls. I realized that I didn't miss the silence of that place.

Now I felt a sudden sense of shame, as though I'd made a terrible mistake without having any idea of what it was. Yes, I'd asked him a question about himself, and I'd genuinely wanted to know the answer. If I really examined my curiosity, I would be able to see that it went very deep. I'd been alone for a long time, and I worried that it showed.

Of course it showed, I thought later that night as I undressed for bed. The room that Harper had given me wasn't particularly large but was certainly pretty, with deep forest green carpeting and a delicate wallpaper pattern of climbing vines that entwined around one another. There was a full-length antique oval mirror on a cherrywood stand, and I stood for a moment in front of it before I pulled on one of my sister's silk nightgowns, critically peering at my reflection, something I hadn't done in a long time. At age thirty-six, my body was still taut and hadn't been pulled or stretched by childbirth or by excess weight. I looked much the way I had when I was twenty-six, or even sixteen: slender, long legs, full breasts. I knew that I was pretty in a muted, understated way, but suddenly I worried that my solitude was visible, that it was written in boldface all over me. I quickly pulled on the pale green night-

∞

gown and stepped into bed, not wanting to dwell on this depressing possibility.

But the morning brought a surprise. I was up early, and I took the newspaper, my cup of coffee, and one of Jeannette's warm biscuits out to the sunroom. I was sitting and having breakfast when the butler, Tom, tall and poker-faced, came and stood in the doorway, holding a cordless telephone in his hand.

"Ms. Mallory, there's a telephone call for you," he said.

I assumed that the call was from someone at the Longwood Falls Library; it sometimes seemed as though I was the only one who understood the new filing system that had been instituted that year. When I picked up the phone, I fully expected to hear the words, "Liz, I'm really sorry to bother you, but we have a filing emergency . . ."

But instead, a man's voice was on the line, familiar in its hesitance and slightly rough edges. "I'm really sorry I was rude yesterday," he said, instead of the usual "hello."

"Excuse me?" I said.

"At the Point," he said. There was a pause. "This is David Fields," he went on. "Nick's teacher."

"Oh. Hello," I said, feeling myself become suffused with awkwardness and excitement. "You weren't rude," I lied. "Not that I noticed."

"Yes, I was," he said. "I obsessed about it all last night. I want a chance to explain."

"There's no need," I said.

"Well, I'd still like to anyway," he said. "It would make me feel better. How about tomorrow night, if that isn't too short notice. Are you by any chance free for dinner?"

I wanted to laugh. Of course, I had no plans; all I did here in Stone Point was spend time with Nick. But David Fields couldn't possibly know that; actually, he knew nothing about me. And I knew nothing about him. I didn't know whether he was seriously involved with someone, or whether he was even married, for his ring finger had been hidden beneath his glove. We were absolute strangers to each other, and he was graciously extending himself to me.

The next night David picked me up at seven in his slightly battered car. I was relieved that he wasn't driving one of the very expensive cars that could be seen all around Stone Point. He was neither wealthy nor flashy; he was a teacher who drove a car that needed a few repairs. This made me feel more at ease. I was wearing a long-sleeved, black wool dress of Harper's. It was the kind of dress that could have been worn to dinner at a four-star restaurant or at an informal coffee shop; I wasn't sure what kind of date this would be. I wasn't even sure if it was a date, actually. I didn't know what to expect now, and so I tried to expect nothing at all.

David Fields got out of his car and stood at the door of Harper's house in the aviator jacket he'd worn when we'd met, but now it was unzipped, revealing a gray turtleneck sweater beneath. He also still wore those cracked leather gloves, and his face was slightly pink from the cold.

"Shall we?" he asked, not coming in any farther than the front hall, with its shining marble tiles.

I said yes, and slipped on my coat. I wasn't comfortable inviting him into my sister's house in her absence, although Nick quickly came down to say hi to his teacher before we left. Jeannette had promised to play Clue with him that evening after she was done in the kitchen, so Nick would be well occupied. He seemed excited to see his teacher in his home, the way any child would.

We drove in relative silence to Scotto's, the Italian restaurant in town where David had made reservations. Occasionally, as we drove, David offered a comment about the condition of the roads, or what a terrific, smart kid Nick was when you were able to break through his shell, or how shocking Doe's death had been to the community, but this was just filler. Finally he gave up, turning on a tape of classical music instead, and we both listened to a violin concerto until we arrived at the restaurant.

The moment we walked into Scotto's I knew this was the kind of place I would have chosen. It was unpretentious, small, and pretty; I couldn't imagine that Harper would have ever wanted to eat here. I knew that her tastes tended to send her to restaurants where the food was carefully arranged on the plate into little sculptures that looked almost too artful to eat. But Scotto's had soothing, basic Italian food: deep bowls of handmade ribbon pasta that gave off the fragrances of butter and garlic. All around us, people were laughing, and the candlelight lent the entire room a warmth and allure. It was the perfect antidote to the winter night that was starting to send snow lashing against the windows of the restaurant.

David and I were led to a booth in the back of the room. The table linen was slightly thin in a couple of spots, but the basket of bread was crusty and delicious, and

David ordered a bottle of red wine, which brought an extra bit of heat to my face and relaxed me a little. I was extremely nervous, I realized, in a way that I hadn't been in years. It was as though I somehow knew that this night was important, that it counted.

David took a sip of his wine and then put the glass down. I could see the hairs on his wrist curling over the edge of his sleeve. "What happened the other day," he finally said in a soft, halting voice, "I'm sorry about it. I know that I got very weird all of a sudden, and you must have thought . . . well, I don't know what you must have thought." He looked at me inquisitively. "Maybe you'll tell me," he said.

"I thought that I'd gotten too personal," I said. "That I was asking you too much about yourself."

David frowned slightly. "Oh no," he said. "That wasn't it. I like when people ask questions. It shows that they're listening. I'm a teacher, remember. I always tell the kids in my class to ask questions constantly, to

∞

plague me with 'why?' and 'how?' " He shook his head. "But when you asked that question about what I was looking for through those binoculars when I was a boy, and you made that joke about the 'mystery woman,' I just closed right up." He took another swallow of wine, as though this was a difficult conversation for him. "What I was looking for, actually," he went on, "*was* kind of a mystery woman. My mother."

"Your mother?" I asked, puzzled. "What do you mean?"

"She drowned when I was six years old," said David. "She just disappeared. It was a mystery, like a lot of drownings. Someone gets a leg cramp, or gets tired, or whatever, and just goes under."

"Oh," I said softly.

"She'd been swimming, and she just never came back. I was completely crushed; I walked around in a daze, feeling like I couldn't breathe. And my father was a wreck; he just went off by himself all the time, and because I was an only child, I had no one. Right after she died, I started spending the day looking through the binoculars. I guess I kept thinking that I'd see her out there, that I'd be the one to find her. There were all these rescue boats circling the area, and helicopters, too. They didn't turn up a thing," he said, shaking his head. "She's still out there somewhere."

The entire time he was speaking, I sat absolutely still. His eyes had a sorrowful quality about them; I could have looked at him all night, I realized, and so I made myself turn away, not wanting to appear to be staring. David's voice was filled with a kind of limitless pain, as though he was still that boy whose mother had been taken from him forever.

Something occurred to me. "Your mother," I said. "Was she that Olympic swimmer, Maggie Thorpe?"

David nodded. "Yes, she was," he said. "You know about that?"

I nodded. "I've read about it," I said.

"Her married name was Fields, my father's name," said David. "But everyone still remembered her from the Olympics, when she was unmarried and known as Maggie Thorpe. So they called her that in all the articles, and the obituaries."

"It had happened a long time ago; the sixties, wasn't it?" I asked.

"Nineteen sixty-five," said David. "August."

"What was she like?" I asked. "Or is that too personal?"

"No, not at all," he said. "When I'm prepared for it, I like talking about it." He took a moment to answer. "For so long I had this *idea* of her," he said. "This made-up idea that was based purely on a little boy's fantasy. I pretended to myself that she was perfect."

"And she really wasn't?"

David smiled. "Well, nobody is, of course. But she came pretty close. She was a terrific mother. She taught me to swim when I was practically a baby. She'd take me in and hold me in her arms, and I would feel the water all around us, but it felt as warm as a bath, because she was there."

We ate as we talked, but though I recall that the food was delicious, I don't remember eating; I was much too involved with listening to what David had to say, and with looking at him—his eyes in the warm, stuttering light of the candles, his mouth.

"The thing with my mother's disappearance," he said, "is that it had one good effect on me. When I got those binoculars, day after day I'd keep looking out over the water for her. But one day I got bored, and I looked upward. I turned the binoculars to the sky. And there I found . . ." His voice trailed off for a second, and he shrugged. "I found something that would wind up being a huge part of my life. The stars." He broke off a piece of bread. "Did you know that I live in an observatory?" he said.

"Is this a joke?" I asked, but he shook his head no.

"I rent a cottage on an estate here in town," David said. "A huge estate called Red Briar.

The owner, an old guy named Boyd, is this total astronomy nut. A long time ago, he built his own observatory on the grounds of the estate, but then he got bored with it and let it fall into disrepair. When I moved in, he paid me to restore the place, and now it's basically mine to use as much as I like. I actually live on the ground floor of the building. Right above me is the telescope. My roof is a giant dome."

I shook my head, amazed. "I can't even picture it," I said.

"Oh, you will," he said quietly. "It's a wonderful place." Then his posture shifted slightly, and he looked down at his hands. "But other than giving me my love of the stars," he said, "my mother's drowning did mostly destructive things to me, of course. It made me very suspicious of people. I always thought they would leave me. I expected them to. And I guess, in a way, it became a self-fulfilling prophecy."

"When you say 'people,' " I said, "do you mean 'women'?"

He nodded, slightly embarrassed, and he pushed a hand through the hair that had fallen in his face.

"Several women, actually," he said. "I went through a string of them during a certain period in my life. I didn't know what I wanted from them, and I probably confused the hell out of them, too. I think I expected them to leave so much that it pushed them away." He paused. "There was one woman in particular," he said. "It was a couple of years ago, and I'm over it now, but I still think about it sometimes." He looked down at his plate, poking at a piece of pasta in the shape of a butterfly. "I thought she was great," he said. "And apparently she thought a lot of me, too. We saw each other all the time. It was obsessive. And then, suddenly . . ." He shrugged. "She was done with me. Decided I wasn't right for her, which I knew meant she was bored. I started having dreams about my mother, which I hadn't done in years. I guess I felt as though I was being abandoned all over again."

"And I guess you were," I said.

He looked at me across the table, our eyes meeting, neither of us turning away. I watched his eyes, his lips, the broad shoulders beneath his sweater, and I felt a surprising wave of feeling cross my body.

"I like talking to you, Liz," he said, and he continued to look steadily at me.

"You seem surprised by that," I said.

"Well, I don't even know you," he said. "I've been talking your ear off during dinner, and you haven't even told me anything about yourself."

"That's all right," I said. "It's not a particularly interesting story."

"No. I want to hear," he said. "I told my story during the appetizer and the main course. So you tell yours during dessert and coffee."

What was there to tell? I wondered. I hadn't been abandoned by a man, and I hadn't had a trauma at an early age, as he had. My parents had died when I was in my twenties, and each death was a sad occurrence but not truly shocking. I told him about how I had loved them, and how, after they were gone, I'd made the decision to stay on in the house where I had grown up.

"That's pretty unusual, isn't it?" he asked. "Being so faithful to what you know. Liking it so much that you want it to continue forever. I guess we have that in common; we've both stayed in the town where we grew up."

I looked away slightly, knowing that it wasn't so much a question of *liking* what my life in Longwood Falls had held as it was of being fearful of trying something new.

"It's more complicated than that," I said uneasily, and then I told him about my sister, and how I'd always known I could never compete with her. "Basically she overshadowed me. She sort of took everything in the world there was to take. I mean, I let her do it, I guess. It worked both ways. But I think I decided it was less painful to settle for a small, unexceptional life, instead of trying for something bigger, flashier. Something like what she has."

∞

"Are those the only options for a life?" David asked. "Small and unexceptional versus big and flashy? There's got to be some other alternative."

"Like what?" I asked.

"Well, how about a happy life?" he said.

"I'm not sure what happiness would mean," I said carefully. "I mean, I have a general understanding of it, but when it comes to what it would feel like—real, uninterrupted happiness—I guess I draw a total blank."

"Me, too," he admitted.

We were eating our dessert now, an Italian cake with dense layers flavored with espresso. I ate slowly, savoring the bitter and the sweet, as well as the fact that I was talking about my life to a man across the table who was listening carefully, as though he was savoring each word I spoke.

What I remember most from that first evening was how we watched each other, each of us studying the other. I also remember all the talking we did. We talked and talked, not as though we had known each other forever, but rather as though we were two people who hadn't known each other until now, and felt the need to make up for lost time. Like me, he was somebody who hadn't opened himself up to many people. He had a handful of good friends, he said, though even with them he tended to hold back a little.

As we talked, I felt so comfortable with him, so relaxed and yet entirely alert to everything that was being said. I remembered the old saying people sometimes used, about how the glass was either half full or half empty, and I thought that it was possible to look at your own life in a similar way: Was my life half over or half begun? Since I'd met David, I really wasn't sure.

"Where did you go?" I heard him asking, and I realized that I'd been momentarily daydreaming, lost in thoughts about this man, and about my own solitary life. I didn't answer him. I saw myself in the library in Longwood Falls, sitting behind my polished wood desk on a sleepy afternoon. Then suddenly, inexplicably, I saw myself in some bed, being kissed by David.

I looked at him across the table. It was anyone's guess where all of this was headed. I was here in Stone Point in order to take care of my sister's son. I was here for that reason only, and I would leave when Harper was strong enough to return. Three hundred miles away was my own house, the heat and lights shut off now, and my own cold bed neatly spread with the pale blue coverlet I'd knitted. My life waited for me back in that town. But across the table was a man with dark eyes and long, beautiful hands. A man whose mother dove into the dark water many years ago and never returned.

I felt an enormous amount for this man; it settled in my face, which was flushed with warmth, and along the length of my body, and in my hands, which couldn't keep still. Surely he didn't feel the same way about me. I realized, as we sat together, that the restaurant had largely cleared out, and that only a few booths were still occupied. Waiters were quietly clearing tables, and a busboy was beginning to mop the floor. Dreamy, late-night music—Sinatra from many decades ago—played on an old jukebox, which pulsed with lights. "Where did you go?" David asked again as the plates were cleared.

"Nowhere," I said. "I'm right here."

Chapter
Four

∞ The morning that holiday break at the Craighead School ended, I got up early to join Nick for breakfast. I found him sitting at the dining room table by himself, a small figure at the far end of a long polished oval as smooth as black ice, reading the back of a cereal box.

"Do you mind?" I asked, pointing to a chair beside him, and Nick shook his head. "What are you reading?"

Nick shrugged.

"May I?" I reached for the cereal box and turned it around so I could see the back. It was covered with brightly colored drawings—riddles, I realized. I read one to myself, then, covering the answer, turned the box so Nick could see it. "Have you done this one yet?" I asked him.

He spooned some cereal and shook his head.

"Okay," I said. "Guess what this is."

Nick placed the spoon back in the bowl and leaned forward, studying the drawing with an impressive level of concentration. The drawing appeared to be a letter *C* with short lines sticking straight away from it like porcupine quills.

"Give up?" I asked.

He looked up at me.

"A centipede doing sit-ups," I read aloud.

At first, nothing. Then, slowly—slowly—a smile formed on Nick's face, almost as if it were emerging despite his best efforts to contain it. This was, I realized, the first time I'd ever seen Nick smile—the first time I'd ever seen him show real pleasure. Usually what he showed, while playing Clue or cross-country skiing, was *appreciation*—a mature understanding of the intricacies of a board game or the mysteries of nature, and not a boyish response in the least.

It was beginning to occur to me that Nick approached everything with this same determination and seriousness of purpose. It was, I thought now as I looked at Nick sitting next to me at the table, dressed for school, a manner that fit a boy in a navy blazer and matching tie over a pale blue buttoned-down Oxford cloth shirt. His hair was damp, his part perfect. If it weren't for the mouthful of multicolored cereal he occasionally revealed, he wouldn't have looked like a child at all. It struck me as odd and sad that my sister, the free spirit, would raise a boy who looked as if he should be addressed as "Master," and I had to wonder: Was Nick so serious because of what had happened to his sister—which was what I'd been assuming? Or was this the way he always was?

"Listen, Nick," I said. "I was wondering. How do you get to school? Bus?"

He shook his head. "No. Tom takes me. The butler."

He said this softly, head bowed, as if at some level he understood how absurd it might sound to me.

"Well," I said, "what would you say if *I* drove you every day? In my slightly dusty car that needs an oil change."

He looked up, and the expression on his face told me that he thought I might be making a joke. Then he said, "Really?" I nodded, but still he looked doubtful.

"I'd like to," I said, "if you'd like me to."

He seemed to be considering the offer. "You'd have to get up early," he said. "My mom says the time of day I have to wake up for school is 'inhuman.' "

"Well," I said, feeling a slight crackle of superiority over my sister, "I don't mind getting up. In fact, I look forward to it."

He thought some more. Then, at last, he said, "All right," but I noticed that he had to glance around first, as though we were breaking some unwritten law.

The Observatory

∞

My main reason for wanting to be with Nick that morning was the same as it always was: to make sure he had someone to talk to, especially on his first day back among his friends after the accident. Still, I can't say it didn't occur to me that I might see David when I dropped Nick off. Since that evening at Scotto's, we'd gotten together once more, this time over dinner at a seafood restaurant with hanging nets. David asked me to tell him more about myself, and as I did he listened fully, and then it was his turn to tell me more about himself, and mine to ask questions, and it all went as effortlessly as the first time. Later, after he'd driven me home, and we were standing together on the gravel drive outside The Eaves, he leaned forward and lightly grazed my cheek with his lips. He paused for a moment, as if he wanted to say something, but then seemed to think better of it. He shoved his hands in his pockets, turned away, and headed back to his car. I watched him go, bewildered and excited and wondering when I would see him again.

Now, a couple of days later, as I turned my car through the tall iron gates of the Craighead School and followed along the driveway to the main building, I couldn't help straining to see over the heads of children chasing one another up the front steps. I don't know what I expected—Mr. Fields, the second-grade teacher, monitoring the front door, I guess. But the person at the door, shaking hands with children as they entered, was a distinguished, silver-haired gentleman in his sixties, the headmaster, presumably. Then I felt Nick watching me.

I smiled quickly. "I'll see you at three," I said, but he didn't move. He kept looking at me, studying me with the same intensity he'd brought to a riddle on the back of a cereal box.

"Thank you for the ride, Aunt Liz," he finally said, and then he grabbed his oversize backpack with various key chains hanging from it, and he was gone.

* * *

∞

I didn't want to go back to The Eaves. The idea of being in that cavernous house without Nick seemed unpleasant. Compared to those empty, endless halls, even the overpriced and disconcertingly well-heeled shops on Horseshoe Lane in Stone Point seemed welcoming. Each store window was filled with items that looked practically edible: brightly colored European leather shoes and handbags with shining gold clasps. I wasn't buying; in each shop I immediately told the saleswoman so. Still, the way they came right over to me and invited me to browse anyway—as if a customer on a Monday morning in the middle of winter was as exotic as an Easter lily surfacing through the snow—made me feel they were grateful for my company. I know I was for theirs. But after I'd made my way from one end of the expensive shopping district to the other before lunch, I couldn't help wondering how I would pass my time the next day, and the day after that.

When lunchtime arrived, I stopped at the

Express Diner next to the train station, and took a booth by the window. I ordered the daily special, today a chicken salad on white toast, and looked out at the tracks that had carried Aunt Leatrice to New York City, and from there up to Longwood Falls. The time was coming when I would have to go back, too, and I felt an odd reluctance to leave. It had to do with David. The two dinners we'd had had been wonderful, and in the quivering glow of the candlelight, anything had seemed possible. But now, staring at the midday glare of cars in the train station parking lot, I wondered if I'd only been kidding myself.

Just before three o'clock, I drove back to the Craighead School to pick up Nick. I pulled my car into the line of vehicles idling in the long driveway, several compact school buses at the front, followed by a fleet of dark sedans. Some mothers had gotten out of their cars to wait together and chat; they were all tall, wealthy-looking women, their hair fashionably styled and streaked, their long legs poking through the bottom of glossy ankle-length fur coats. They were like Harper—like Harper used to be, anyway—sexually desirable, restless women with energy and entitlement. As I watched them, I couldn't help thinking of David, the handsome, unmarried second-grade teacher.

I knew it was absurd to feel jealous; there was nothing to base this feeling on except a vague stirring of possessiveness that I had no right to feel. Still, as I sat in the overheated front seat, an oldies station playing song after song from my teenage years, I could imagine one of these women borrowing David as she might a handyman or gardener—someone good-looking and strong to occupy a few lonely hours and provide the kind of rough physical pleasure that their own distracted businessmen husbands no longer did. But I couldn't imagine any of these women appreciating the man I alone had discovered over dinner—the modest, wounded, and gently handsome David.

And then there he was, knocking on the

passenger window, jarring me from my thoughts about him.

"I'm sorry I scared you," he said when I'd rolled down the window. "I've been on the front steps waving to you, trying to get your attention, but you seemed lost in thought."

"How did you know I was here?" I asked.

"Nick told me," said David. "He'll be out in a minute, but I wanted to talk to you first."

"Is something wrong?" With a sickening swoop, I suddenly remembered my real reason for being in Stone Point: to protect Nick, to be the mother he didn't have right now. Had his first day back at school somehow been too upsetting?

"No, no," David said. "Nick's fine. Everything's fine." He paused, then added, "Everything's more than fine, I think."

Vapor was pouring from David's mouth with each breath, and I suddenly noticed he was coatless. The only thing between David and the cold was a blue denim shirt, its sleeves rolled halfway up his forearms, and a loosely knotted tie, in deference to Craighead's dress code.

"My God," I said, "you must be freezing. Get in the car."

He shook his head. "I'm used to the cold," he said. "Nights in the observatory, you know. But listen." He briefly looked toward the group of women I'd been watching. Then he leaned closer, through the open window. "I've really been having a nice time with you," he said, his voice lower now.

"Me, too," I told him.

"Those dinners, those conversations—they mean a lot," he said.

"I feel the same way," I said. I found myself glancing back at the other women, and saw that in fact they *were* looking at us. What could they think they were seeing but the teacher of a boy whose sister had just died, speaking with intensity to a woman who bore a strong family resemblance to that boy's mother?

"Are you busy Friday night?" David asked.

"I was thinking maybe you could come over to my cottage at Red Briar. Around eight? I'll fix some dinner, and we could head up to the observatory. If you're interested, that is."

"I am," I said quietly.

"Well, that's great," said David. One of the women, I noticed then, had broken away from the others and was walking our way. In a loud voice, David quickly began to improvise. "And I think he's doing fine," he said. "He's a great kid; we'll be looking out for him. I don't think you have to worry." Then he turned around and swiftly headed back to the school, his tie flapping up over his shoulder like a wing.

The rest of the week passed effortlessly, dreamily, and I had no trouble finding something to occupy my days. I drove Nick to school, I returned to Horseshoe Lane a couple of times and actually bought myself an expensive blouse to wear to dinner on Friday, and then I walked up and down the street until I'd settled on shoes and a handbag to match. These were extravagances, but I allowed myself to buy them, knowing they were connected to David, to wanting to look good for him.

I also explored the Stone Point Library, a big, imposing building on the water, introduced myself to the elderly head librarian there, and picked up some pointers on correcting the cataloguing problems back in Longwood Falls. And I even stopped at Harper's house a few times, to fix myself a quick lunch over the protests of Jeannette, who wasn't used to having other people working in her kitchen.

But it was the promise of Friday night that illuminated the entire week for me. If it turned out the way I thought it might, then it would be one of those times that forever divide a life, paring it cleanly into a before and after.

This hope was an unfair burden to place on any occasion, but I was no longer a young girl living under the illusion of immortality, a life stretching endlessly ahead, full of infinite possibility. Life was short. Maybe it wasn't always as short as David's mother's life, interrupted by a swimming accident; and it certainly was rarely as short as Doe's. But even for the luckiest, life wasn't something to be squandered. I was thirty-six—old enough to be jaded, but still young enough to think that I didn't need to be. There was a chance at love, perhaps a last chance, and it waited inside an observatory in the middle of winter. Without having expressly said so, David and I both wanted answers, and we hoped we could get them in whatever time remained, before Harper came home and the clock struck midnight and my ballgown turned back into rags.

Friday morning I informed Jeannette that I wouldn't be having dinner at home that night. Friday evening I dressed in the outfit I'd spent the week piecing together, but as I appraised myself in the standing full-length mirror in a corner of my room, I saw that something was missing. Then I knew what it was. I headed for my sister's room, to the dressing room I'd visited several times in the previous weeks. There I confronted Harper's collection of silk scarves, each hanging on its own brass hook. I plucked a gold scarf free and quickly knotted it, tucking one end behind my hair, letting the other drop easily. And then I turned toward the standing full-length mirror in a corner of my sister's room, identical to the mirror in my room, and considered the twin I saw there, looking back at me, and I was reminded again of the truth about Harper and me that I always knew: Nobody would ever have trouble telling the two of us apart. But I also tried to see myself now for what I was, to see myself through David's eyes. *Ready or not,* I thought, and then I corrected myself.

Ready.

David's cottage was located on an estate five miles away from Harper's. There were several buildings behind the red stone mansion, but it was easy to tell which was David's: his was the one with the round roof.

As I got out of my car and walked up to the door of the cottage, I could see him through the window, slicing something on a cutting board in the kitchen, his brow furrowed with effort, his shoulders moving with the rhythm of the strokes. I knew I shouldn't, but I stopped and continued to watch him for a moment, maybe to steal a secret glimpse of David, or maybe just to prolong the moment before I crossed that threshold. Then, I knocked.

After a moment, the door opened. David, holding a bottle of red wine by its neck and a Swiss Army knife with its corkscrew open, smiled at me. He stepped outside, onto the gravel of the drive, brushed my cheek with the lightest kiss, and then looked up.

"Good," he said, nodding to himself.

I followed his gaze. The sky was clear; many stars were out.

"Possibly very good," David went on. "We'll see." And he held his arm out, indicating that I should precede him inside.

The cottage was really only one big circular room. The kitchen that I'd glimpsed through the window occupied half of the front section, and a low beige couch and wooden coffee table the other half. There were striking landscape photographs on the walls and an Oriental rug with a complex design on the floor. The place was strange and beautiful and snug; it seemed utterly private and unusual and away from the rest of the world.

"It's wonderful," I said with genuine feeling, and David seemed pleased.

But then I noticed something that I couldn't figure out. In the middle of the room was a huge structure that ran from floor to ceiling. It was concrete, bare, and followed the curve of the outer wall. I stood for a moment and puzzled over it.

"You noticed," said David.

"Well, I couldn't exactly miss it," I said. I crossed to get a closer look. This structure, this wall, was made of cement blocks fitted together. Slowly I walked around it, David following behind.

"This," he explained, "is the base of the telescope." As I walked around it, I passed from the front part of the cottage to the back, which was occupied by a neatly made bed with a Mexican comforter across it, and a handsome old schoolteacher's desk strewn with papers. "It goes down another ten feet or so," David said. "Right into bedrock."

"I'm impressed," I said.

"Telescopes are really sensitive," he said, "especially ones this size. They'll pick up the tiniest vibration." He came closer. "The railroad, which runs a couple of hundred feet from here. Your car pulling up. Me, walking around down here." He slapped the concrete with the flat of his hand, and it made a fleshy, echoless sound. "But this won't budge," he said.

"It's sort of like living in a lighthouse," I told him, running one of my hands along the concrete. The surface was pebbly and cool.

"More than you know," he said. He held up the bottle. "Want some wine?" he asked. I nodded, and he gripped the Swiss Army corkscrew, eased it in, and began twisting. "It's not just the shape of the place," he said, "the roundness of it. It's the feel of it, too. It's what happens here. In a lighthouse, you're at land's end, looking out across the water. Up in the observatory, it's the same thing, except you're at the ends of the earth, and the sea you're looking across is space. The universe. Everything there is that isn't you. This sounds kind of odd," he suddenly added, growing self-conscious and looking down at the bottle.

"No," I said. "It doesn't."

He shrugged anyway, pulling the cork free. Then he turned to the counter and quickly poured two glasses of wine. "It's just that up there, in the observatory," he said, "it's easy to forget about everything else." He handed me a glass and picked up one for himself. "You're all alone. It's just you. You and . . . whatever."

I raised my glass. "To 'whatever,' then," I said.

We toasted lightly. Then I noticed that

something about me seemed to have caught his eye.

"That scarf," he said. "It's really nice."

He reached out and gently lifted the end of it that hung down from my neck. It figured. The one thing about me that he had singled out for a compliment was my sister's contribution to the ensemble. The things that I'd chosen on my own at an overpriced shop in Stone Point could never be good enough; it had to be an accessory of hers that I'd added, on a moment's notice, that provided the magic touch.

Yet, oddly, it did provide it. It easily might not have. I might have resisted, I might have allowed David's careless compliment to ruin the evening, might have resented Harper for yoking me with yet another reminder of what she'd always meant to me, and what she'd always mean.

But when David lifted the end of the scarf off my neck, his fingers brushed the skin there, and I felt a charge, an almost electrical kind of response. In that moment, it didn't matter that the one thing about me he'd seen fit to praise wasn't of my own choosing. I stood and I took his compliment. I accepted his admiration. I held perfectly still while David ran the gold silk between two fingers. I don't think I even breathed until he let the scarf slip away. We looked at each other, the moment over for now.

"So when does the show begin?" I asked nervously, breaking the silence. "The star show, I mean."

"Whenever you like," he said softly. "We could go up now."

This last statement seemed to be more of a question. I nodded hesitantly. David took the wineglass from me and placed it on the counter. I vaguely took in the dinner he'd been preparing: the oiled wooden salad bowl full of torn greens, the pounded chicken breasts lying on a plate, the onions he'd been slicing into careful, thin circles when I'd watched him through the window. "Here," David said. "You'll need this."

I turned to find him holding my coat. I

slipped one arm into it, then the other. "What about you?" I asked.

"I'll be fine," he said, pointing to his soft, royal blue fisherman's sweater.

And then David did a remarkable thing, something I couldn't remember any other man ever doing before: he offered me his hand. It was an oddly formal gesture, but his smile neutralized it somehow, recast it as an awkward yet necessary part of the show that was just beginning. I accepted his hand.

"This way," he said, and he began to lead me around the circular wall, but before we reached the back of his cottage, he opened a door in the outer wall that I hadn't noticed before. He cautioned me to watch my step, and then he led me up a metal spiral staircase, into darkness. When we reached the landing, David suggested we wait a moment for my eyes to adjust.

Slowly, I began to see that something was looming over us, and in a moment I could make out what it was: the silhouette of the telescope against the night sky. And then I could see the outline of the opening in the dome. I felt David's hand reaching for mine.

"Here," he said. "Watch your step." He led me several paces over, then one step up. Then he released my hand, turned me by the shoulders so that I was facing him, and reached behind me. "Here," he said again.

I turned. Very dimly I could distinguish a lump of darkness against a deeper darkness. After a moment, it seemed to assume the shape of a seat—rather, two seats, side by side, like a porch swing.

"The observer's chair," he said.

I sat down. The seat was cushioned and comfortable. Then David sat beside me and said, "Ready?"

"Ready," I said, though I wasn't sure for what.

David leaned forward and gripped something resting between us that I could barely make out. Something round. He began turning it, and I seemed to understand it was a steering wheel of sorts, and as he rotated it to the left, another amazing thing happened: We rose.

Without meaning to, I let out a light whoop. "Sorry," I said, raising my hand to my lips.

"Don't be. Let it out. Why not?" David said.

The seat appeared to be on some sort of gear and pulley system; by turning the wheel, he made it advance along a set of tracks that took us both back and up. Suddenly the whole experience—the cottage downstairs, the observatory upstairs, and now a ride, of all things—struck me as so absurd that I wanted to keep laughing, but I suppressed it.

"This is an exact replica of the observatory at Harvard, only smaller," David said. "The original dates from the eighteen forties. When Old Man Boyd decided he just had to have an observatory on his property, he wanted one like the one he knew from

his school days. If it was good enough for
Harvard . . ." His voice trailed off. He let go
of the wheel and turned to me. "Would you
like to drive?" he asked.

And so I did. I held the wheel and worked
it to the left until we came to a jarring stop
at the top of this contraption, which made
me whoop again, and apologize again, and
made David tell me not to apologize again,
and by then we were both laughing so hard
I turned the wheel back over to him, and he
worked it to the right and we lurched forward and began our descent.

Halfway down, David stopped. "Now
here's the good part," he said, reaching out
in the darkness for the end of the telescope.
He sat up straighter, leaned forward, and
pressed into the eyepiece. "I set this up earlier, and if you give me a moment—" He began wheeling to the right again, lowering
the seat farther, but he didn't remove his eye
from the telescope. "We got here earlier
than I thought we would. I thought we'd eat

first. So what I'm looking for now is still a little higher in the sky than I expected." He stopped wheeling. "There. There it is." David pulled away from the eyepiece. "Now I want you to see this," he told me. "But don't touch anything or you'll knock it out of whack. Just gently, here, lean forward, like this—"

I did as he said. First, walking up the twisting stairs and into this dark room, letting David lead me by the hand, and now, leaning forward to peer into the telescope— it was as though he'd told a child he had a surprise, and to close her eyes, and suddenly: Open them!

"Do you see it?" he asked me with quiet excitement.

"Oh," was all I could say.

It was Saturn—the same Saturn we'd seen together the first day we met, out on the Point. But now, under the much greater magnification of this massive telescope, the planet leaped to life: the swirls of gray and gold on the surface, the silver rings, and somehow the whole miraculous sight suspended in the dark.

"It's just the most beautiful thing," I said.

"I wanted you to see that," said David. His voice was a whisper now. "To see what you were missing last time."

I turned from the eyepiece. His face was close to mine. My eyes had adjusted so that I could make out his. Was he seeing the desire in mine that I was seeing in his? I turned my face upward, under his, and the last thing I remember seeing as I closed my eyes was his dark silhouette moving into place over me, obscuring the sky, eclipsing the heavens.

His hands were inside my coat, as if trying to find warmth. He was gently touching my shoulders, my collarbone, my breasts. And I reached beneath his sweater, touched him along his chest, feeling the smooth planes of muscle. I wanted this to go on and on, to last for years. I wanted us to stay suspended in this place, in this soft, swaying chair under the stars themselves. I could feel my hips shifting on the cushion as I pulled him closer. I shifted again, and David was upon me. He ran his hands down my skirt and then began sliding them upward. I raised my own hands to hold his shoulders, and in the dark I felt them moving with the same rhythm I'd seen him using through his kitchen window with the knife.

David seemed to be both absolutely lost in the moment and yet concentrating very hard, too; he was with me entirely, and I'd never felt that with anyone before, and I doubted I'd ever feel it with anyone else. This sort of thing didn't happen very often, and I knew that David knew it, too. It was like a comet, one of those comets that only comes around once in a lifetime, so you'd better know exactly where and when to look.

Later, we lay on Old Man Boyd's observer's chair, silent except for our gradually slowing breathing. David's chin rested against my shoulder. Then I felt him lift his head and gaze at me in the dark.

"Okay," he said. "You can open your eyes."

Chapter
Five

∞ We were scared; we'd have been crazy not to be. What was happening to us was so sudden, so complete, that we almost didn't have time to think about it. After that first time together in the observatory, we shakily descended the circular metal staircase. I sat in a chair wearing David's oversize flannel robe while he cooked the chicken and whisked a mustard dressing for the salad that he'd been preparing when I'd arrived, and then we went to bed. This time we proceeded with each other more slowly. We lingered under the bright zigzags of the Mexican comforter, beginning to learn the touch and the taste of a new partner, to understand the particulars of another person's pleasure and response.

Later, we lay and talked softly. At one point, David said that we ought to give his cottage a name.

"It's only fair," he said. "All the houses around here have names; why not mine?"

And so we ironically christened his cottage Stardust, laughing as we did, sharing another giddy moment together. Then we slept for a while, and woke up again a while later, simply lying wide awake in the dark but saying nothing.

Outside the window I could see a midwinter sky packed full of stars. Just as David had said earlier in the evening, it was easy to be in this place and imagine that we were totally on our own out here. He'd been talking then about the observatory upstairs, but it was equally true downstairs as well. Or maybe that was just an illusion that all new lovers share: that there's nobody else, nothing else, just you and me, and not even that anymore: just us.

"I see what you mean," I said at one point, "about this being the end of the world."

He had one arm thrown back behind his head, exposing the thatch of hair under it. "Not 'end of the world,' Liz," he said. " 'Ends of the earth.' "

I ran a finger along David's chest. "Well, you know what I mean," I said.

He took a long time to respond, and when he did he didn't look at me. "Maybe you were right the first time," he said. "That's what it can be like, when you really feel things for somebody and it doesn't work out."

"I guess I wouldn't know about that," I said softly. I thought of Jeff, back in Longwood Falls, all those years ago. We'd ended the relationship and he'd moved away. I hadn't broken his heart, and he hadn't broken mine. No one had; I hadn't let anyone come that close.

At last David turned toward me and said, "I hope you never find out." Then we said nothing more about it.

Late that night I left David's house and went back to The Eaves. When I looked into

Nick's room, I saw that he was still fast asleep, his mouth open, his face flushed. I walked to his bed and impulsively kissed his forehead, feeling a surge of tenderness for this little boy, a sensation that somehow had increased since last night, when I'd been with David. It was as though love—or the promise of it—brought out other kinds of love. I loved David and I loved Nick; I was excited and thrilled and wished I could have told this little boy, "I'm in love with your teacher," but I knew I shouldn't. What David and I had was too raw, too fragile to be examined in this way, or spoken about. I would keep it to myself.

I spent that morning with Nick, playing board games and putting together a model World War II airplane with him until my fingers were stuck together with glue. Later, a friend of his from school was coming over, a boy named Zachary, and I was glad Nick would be with someone his own age, someone, maybe, with whom he could be more

∞

open. But for now, we sat quietly, and even as I concentrated hard on attaching the delicate wings of Nick's fighter plane, my thoughts were partially circling what had happened last night in David's cottage. I understood that part of what had brought us together so breathlessly was that we were already running out of time. Under other circumstances, we might have been able to get to know each other slowly over weeks, months, years even—whatever it took to discover each other fully and decide whether we were compatible. But the fact was, we didn't have the luxury of time; soon my sister would be home and I was supposed to head back to Longwood Falls.

When I was with David, I found myself experiencing everything in a way I never had before. Which was why, when David and I lay in bed again the next time, and he sat up on his elbow and said, "Listen, Liz, we have to talk about something," I froze in place. Oh, I thought, my stomach tightening, here it comes. We'd been lovers for a matter of days, and now I was hearing the words that, this early in a relationship, can mean only one thing: *This isn't working.* And in that moment, my world fell away.

But what David said was, "I'm going to Hawaii next weekend to see the observatories there. This is a trip I've been planning for a long time. It was hard finding time to get away, and obviously it's not the ideal moment, but the school is letting me use a couple of my teacher's resource days, and my travel agent worked out this great package for me, and I've been saving up for it. And it's very important to me."

"Okay," I heard myself say, still not sure where this conversation was going.

"The observatories there are nothing like this observatory here," he said. "They're the real deal, some of the biggest in the world. Anyway, the point is that I've still got this airline mileage that I've been saving up for something important, and I was thinking, this is it. If you wanted to go with me, I

∞

thought it might be a chance for us to get away together."

My relief was palpable, and came out in a big, involuntary sigh.

"What is it?" David asked.

"Nothing," I said. "I just thought you were getting ready to tell me something else. To tell me you didn't think we should see each other anymore."

"No, no," he said. "It's the opposite. I thought this would be a chance for us to get away together, really get away."

I waited a moment. Then I said, "Yes."

"Yes, what?"

"I'll go with you. I mean, assuming that Harper says it's okay. Jeannette's there, and Nick will be in good hands, and it's only for a few days, but I'll have to ask."

David sank back on his pillow, smiling with sleepy contentment. "I hope she says yes," he said. Then he turned to me, and in a quiet voice he said, "I love you, Liz."

I waited, letting the words shimmer for an extra moment, actually feeling them as though they were tactile, real. "I love you, too," I told him, my voice quiet, too, and suddenly hoarse.

"Are you scared?" he asked.

I nodded. "You?"

"Yes," he said. "Very."

We barely knew each other, and had spent only two nights together, yet it seemed that we'd already come a great distance. We'd agreed that what we wanted more than anything else was to travel far away and focus solely on each other in a way we couldn't here in Stone Point, even in the hideaway of Stardust, David's cottage. For a few days, forget about Nick. Forget about Harper. Forget about the Craighead School and the Longwood Falls Public Library. Forget about everybody and everything but us.

Whatever else it might turn out to be, the trip to Hawaii was our first chance to be a couple—not just for a few hours by ourselves every night, but all the time, in front of the world. We'd depart for the islands as a couple, we'd travel as a couple, and, if all went well, we'd return as one, too, and try to figure out what that meant, and how to make it work long-distance.

The next day, I called Harper while Nick was out of the house and asked her permission. I had anticipated some surprise on her part that I'd gotten involved with someone, perhaps even mild shock that it was Mr. Fields, her son's teacher; but, in the end, I guess I expected her blessing. What I got instead was silence, a discomfort that was impossible to miss even over the length of telephone wire that connected us. And I realized that I'd been insensitive. Here was Harper, overwhelmed by grief, barely able to think about anything but how to get through the day, and here was her sister, asking for permission to go to Hawaii with a lover.

"That's great, Liz," she finally said softly. "Yes, by all means, go."

"Are you sure? You don't think it's weird?"

"Weird how?" she asked after a long moment.

"Well, because he's Nick's teacher," I said.

Another pause, and then: "I'm happy for you, Liz. Really."

That evening, I told Nick I was thinking of going away for a few days. He and I were playing Clue on the family room rug. As I talked to Nick, he didn't look up from the game board; instead, he started fidgeting with the pile of game-piece weapons. He picked up the tiny lead pipe and poked it against the board.

"I'll be going to Hawaii," I told him. "With Mr. Fields."

Now Nick looked up. "My teacher?" he said, as if we knew some other Mr. Fields.

"That's right. You know I've been spending a lot of time with him."

"Can I come?" he asked.

"No, I don't think that's possible," I said.

Nick turned away sharply, throwing down the toy lead pipe and not saying anything.

The intensity of his reaction surprised me, and for a moment I didn't know how to respond. Since I'd been staying at the house, he'd seemed to accept my presence in a quiet, guarded fashion. But now I realized that I didn't know what he really felt about me; somehow, I'd missed something here, something crucial.

"Well, I just won't go to Hawaii then," I said. "I'm so sorry, Nick. I had no idea it would upset you that much if I went away for a few days. But no, you're right, I'll definitely—"

"It's not that. It's not Hawaii."

His voice was thin. His back was to me. I could see his shoulders hunching, his neck straining with the effort not to burst into tears.

"All right, then," I said, after a moment. "What is it?"

"You're going away for good soon, aren't you?" he asked.

"You mean back to Longwood Falls?" He nodded his head. "Well, I'm supposed to, when your mom is strong enough to come home," I stammered.

I reached out to touch his shoulder, but he jerked away.

"Look, Nick," I tried, "things are confusing right now. I told you all along that I'd be leaving when your mom returns. I have a life up in Longwood Falls. Friends. A job. Aunt Leatrice." I could see his shoulders begin to shudder, and I heard a gasp escape as he continued his struggle against the tears. "Oh, Nick," I went on, reaching out to him again, but again he pulled away, standing up abruptly. "Nick, listen to me."

"No!" he said, and he put his hands over his ears. I got up and circled around him, and when he began to turn away again I grabbed his shoulder and got down on my knees and tried to look him in the eyes. But Nick only stared through me as if I weren't there, as if I'd already left, one more ghost in a life already overcrowded with them.

"All right then, don't listen," I said, "but I'm going to keep talking anyway, because I think you ought to hear this. When I go back to Longwood Falls, we'll talk on the phone, and I'll E-mail you lists of books I think you'll like, and I'll drive down to visit you. And you can even come up to stay with me, in the house where your mom and I grew up. I promise you, we'll always be friends, no matter what happens. I promise."

Something crossed his face then—a look of surrender—and the tears came at last. He put his hands down and collapsed against me, and I could feel his face moving wetly against my shoulder, his head nodding. I'd never seen Nick cry before. A few days earlier at the breakfast table, I'd realized I was seeing him smile for the first time, and now I realized I was seeing him cry for the first time, and at the moment I couldn't say which was a more hopeful sign. And then I realized that I could have cried right then, too. I held Nick and talked to him for a long time, and when I had nothing to say, I still held on until the sobbing stopped.

Finally he was quiet, and then he fell

asleep in my arms. I must have fallen asleep, too, for the next thing I remember, he was shaking me awake, saying, "Aunt Liz, Aunt Liz?"

"What is it?" I asked, disoriented.

"I want you to go," he said.

"What?" I said, coming fully out of sleep, recalling the first day we'd met, out on the hill, and how he'd said the same thing then.

But now he was saying, "I mean, I want you to go to Hawaii, and bring me back a piece of a volcano, okay?"

I sat up straighter and looked at him. "I thought we decided I wasn't going," I said.

"Well," said Nick, "I think you should. I really want a piece of a volcano. My friend Zachary will be so jealous." But I knew that his desire for me to go on this trip had very little to do with volcanic rock. Though only seven years old, Nick was perceptive about other people. He saw how much I really wanted to be alone with David. "It's only for a few days," Nick added. "I'll be fine. Go, Aunt Liz. *Go.*"

The Observatory

∞

*   *   *

From the airplane heading into the Hawaiian Islands, I could see the sun blazing down from overhead, slanting light on an amazing expanse of turquoise water. David and I held hands as the plane touched down at the airport in the middle of the day. True to form, local women festooned us with leis when we arrived—not the plastic kind, but real ones, made of fragrant pink plumeria flowers that smelled unlike anything I'd ever smelled before. As we walked across the tarmac, the heat was strong, and I felt overdressed in my coat. We'd taken off in the middle of winter, and seemingly landed in the middle of summer. I was expecting this, but still the change was startling. David put his arm around me, both of us exhausted from the trip, and nervous about being together so intensely, so far from anything that felt familiar.

When we arrived at our hotel in Hilo, a city located on what's known as the Big Island, a bellboy showed us to our suite, which was decorated in pastel tones and had a balcony that overlooked the white sand of the beach. We stood out on the balcony for a little while, feeling the breeze ripple across us and watching the swimmers play in the water below. I was tired and jet-lagged, but I wanted to see everything all at once, to do everything while I was here. I watched as several children ran into the waves, laughing. I imagined that one of those children was ours, and the daydream was vivid, believable.

Now David took me by the shoulder and turned me toward him. "So here we are, Liz," he said quietly.

"It feels so strange," I said. I looked at him. "Are you growing a beard?" I asked, and he reached up to the field of stubble on his chin.

"I forgot to shave before we left," he admitted.

"I like it," I said.

"Well, I don't think the headmaster of the Craighead School would agree with you," he said. "But for the next four days, it's all yours."

I ran my hand along the roughness of his face, feeling as though I had a claim over that face, which was a sensation unknown to me.

He came forward and we kissed, and then we went inside, letting our clothing drop into soft piles and looking at each other with shyness in the daylight of the hotel room.

"You're so beautiful," David said, coming closer to embrace me. We stood together in the center of that pretty room, and after a few moments David left me and went into the bathroom. I heard the sound of water running; was he taking a shower? But when I went to see what was going on, I found that he had filled the oversize marble whirlpool bath, and that he was waiting for me.

Together we stepped into the heated, scented water. After we settled ourselves in, we moved together and began to kiss, to touch each other in the warm slide of the bath. His new beard was slightly harsh against my face, a contrast to the softness of his hands and the gentle heat of the water. He moved against me, and in the wall-size mirror across the bathroom, I caught a glimpse of David's back, the long line of it, muscled and arched, and of my arms, holding him tightly.

After a while we left the bath and moved to the bed. The sheets were soft white linen, and later we lay entwined in them, in each other, not wanting to move. Eventually, David got up and brought us a can of pineapple juice from the minibar, flipping open the pop-top. We passed it back and forth, drinking thirstily, and though I'd never particularly liked pineapple juice before, it tasted sweet and cool now, and I knew that he'd chosen it as a symbol of our trip, our entry into this exotic land where spiky pineapples improbably grew on trees, where the beach sand was as fine as flour, and where our time belonged only to us.

Eventually I drifted off. In the middle of that first night in Hawaii, I woke up not knowing where I was or what time it was or what day it was. I was alone in the unfamiliar bed. Then I saw a light coming from under the door to the adjoining sitting room. I stood, concerned, and walked through the bedroom, opening the door. There I found him sitting on the couch, looking through some brochures about the Hawaiian observatories. "Hi," I said. "Everything okay?"

"Come sit with me," he said, but I was too tired, and I went back to bed, once again amazed at David's energy, his concentration, his restlessness that awakened him in the middle of the night and made him start thinking about the heavens.

The next morning we set out for the observatories. I was walking out of our hotel room in a pair of shorts and a T-shirt when David called to me.

"Here," he said. "You'll need this."

He was handing me my coat. I started to reach for it, then stopped, figuring it was some sort of joke.

"Trust me," he said.

∞

I considered for a moment. Then I nodded, accepted the coat, and we were off. The road to the mountain was long and curious. Minutes outside Hilo the gentle vegetation abruptly ended, replaced by cactuses.

"We're in the desert," I said incredulously, as we drove on.

To one side of the road in the distance rose Mauna Loa, which David had explained to me was an active volcano. I could see steam venting from it here and there, and to the other side of the road rose its nearly identical twin, Mauna Kea, a dormant volcano and our destination for the day. They were like Harper and me, I thought to myself. Twins who were entirely different.

"Where are you taking me?" I asked.

"You'll see," was all he would say.

I felt the way I had when I was back in his cottage, and it was our first night together, and David was leading me by the hand into the darkness of the observatory. And just as I did that night when I found myself in the observer's chair of the telescope, I trusted him.

I now leaned back in the front seat of our rented four-wheel-drive vehicle and decided to go along for the ride.

Every few minutes, the landscape changed. For a while, it was the ashen, uninterrupted black of volcanic residue. Then we turned, and the road rose, and we were surrounded by rolling green hills. Then the view vanished as we drove upward through clouds, and when we came out of the clouds, the hillside was covered with twiglike shrubs and the occasional bush. I thought of Nick, and his appreciation of nature, and how I'd have to call him that evening to see how he was and tell him that Hawaii had even more places to explore than the grounds of The Eaves, and that someday I'd bring him here and we'd explore it together. Finally David and I came to a stop at what appeared to be a chalet. We climbed out of the car, and to my surprise the air was bracing, even cold.

"I see what you mean," I said, grabbing my coat from the backseat.

David only smiled.

"So where are the telescopes?" I asked.

David pointed past me. I turned; the mountain rose behind me.

"There's more?" I said.

"Yes," he said. "This is where we can acclimate ourselves. We're already at nine thousand feet, and the summit's nearly fourteen thousand." He turned toward the chalet. "And this is where the astronomers stay. Hold on a minute." Before I could say another word, David had trotted off. A tall, gray-haired man was leaving the chalet for the parking lot, and David walked right up to him, said something, and shook his hand. I got back into the car and watched as the two men fell into an instant conversation, nodding their heads, eyeing the sky together.

After a few minutes David climbed back into the car, dropped it into gear, and pulled out of the parking lot. As he steered us onto the winding gravel road to begin the final stretch up the mountain, he was shaking his head and smiling to himself. He was somewhere else now, and I simply watched him, waiting for him to return to earth.

"Do you know who that was?" he finally said, and then he mentioned some name I'd never heard of, and he explained that this was a very important astronomer who had made some important discoveries I'd never heard of either. But I got the idea. He was a hero of sorts to David, someone who had looked into the far reaches of the universe and found things nobody else had ever dreamed of. As David kept on describing for me what this astronomer had accomplished, it occurred to me that I'd never before seen him so excited, so animated, so alive—and it troubled me in a way, because the man I saw in that moment wasn't the one I knew.

So we still had a way to go, then, in order to know each other as deeply as we could. We'd covered a lot of ground in our short time together, but we still had a lot further to travel. Which was only natural for two strangers who'd met for the first time so recently. But what troubled me wasn't simply that David had a side to him that I couldn't reach; it was that I didn't know if I ever would.

The last time we'd been together in his bed in the cottage, lying beneath the Mexican blanket, we'd made love and then sat up and talked for a while, and then we'd gotten mocha chip ice cream out of the freezer and spooned it directly from the carton. I had a little while longer to spend before returning home to Nick, and I'd assumed David and I would spend it together. But suddenly he eased himself out of bed, as if his mind were elsewhere, as if he still had more to do. "Where are you going?" I asked him gently in the dark, although I already knew the answer.

"The observatory."

He'd said it matter-of-factly, and, of course, it was a matter of fact. But the word came to mean more to me than that circular room over our heads. I understood that it was his refuge, the place where he apparently felt more at home than any other, where he could lose himself in a way he couldn't even with me. He pulled on a sweater and a pair of pants and work boots, and walked up the steel staircase. A minute later I heard the rolling thunder of the dome opening, and then the rattle of chains as the ancient pulleys of the observer's chair churned away, straining to raise and lower him. I lay staring out the window for a while, seeing the same sky that David was seeing, yet knowing I wasn't.

But the observatory had become a refuge for me as well. It was a place unlike any I'd ever been: a place where we looked at the heavens, where we made love, where we talked about the universe and each other in reverential whispers.

Now we were a long way from that place we jokingly called Stardust. The Hawaiian landscape was changing yet again. Gone now were the grasslands, the gentle hills, even the scraggly shrubs. We were above the tree line; there was no vegetation here near the top of the mountain, only great gray boulders and slabs, as barren as Mars. And still we climbed. We'd round a bend and the sun would be there, directly before us, blinding us for a moment, and the car would slow, and then David would adjust and we'd press on.

We rode in silence for a while, whether because of the view or the altitude I can't say. My breath came shorter, and a dull ache began hammering somewhere at the back of my neck. My thoughts began scattering, disconnecting and reconfiguring in unpredictable patterns, like a kaleidoscope. It was as if they were putting on a show for my benefit, and I leaned back in the front seat and watched. I watched the road; I watched my thoughts. The gray of the rocks was replaced by white—smooth, unbroken, as blinding as the sun. I thought about the slip of the tongue I'd made back in David's bed, when I'd called his observatory the end of the world, not the ends of the earth. But surely *this* was the end of the world.

"Snow," I said. "In Hawaii."

And then before I could finish puzzling out this sight, we rounded one last bend, and suddenly the top of the mountain came into view, and with it the domes of the observatories, one after another, whiter even than the snow. We cruised past a couple, then a couple more. Finally David stopped the car on a ledge overlooking . . . what? I couldn't say. I climbed out of the car, pulled the belt on my coat tight, and walked to the lip.

Clouds, I guess, only they were far below us now. It was hard to tell where the snow ended and the clouds began; where the clouds broke and the ocean poked through. This blur of sky and earth and water stretched forever in every direction, as if there were no directions anymore, as if we'd left the points of the compass behind us. And maybe we had. It was just us now—the sun, too, settling into a reddish haze at the horizon to one side of us, and nightfall rushing up on us from the other side, the stars just starting to emerge, and the observatories, of course, their domes open now and pivoting slowly, preparing to take aim at some unknowable truth.

But mostly it was us out there in the gathering darkness.

Just us. Nothing but us.

David was standing with his hand on his hips, mouth slightly open, head tipped back like a turkey in a downpour.

"Tell me something," I said. "Tell me what you see."

He took a breath, then said, "Where to begin? Okay. All right. Up there, see where I'm pointing, that bright star? That's—"

"No," I said softly. "Not the names of stars or constellations. Not now."

"Oh," he said. He was silent a long time, not taking his eyes off the sky. "Okay," he finally said. "Here's what I think." He spread his arms, as if waiting for something to fall out of the sky, and if it had, I don't think I would have been surprised. The sun had slipped beyond the horizon now; the sky had finished turning colors and was settling into a deep, enduring black. "Some people look at all this and they go, 'Wow.' I understand that. Who wouldn't? Especially when you know what it is you're looking at, when you begin to understand the distances you're seeing and what they mean. So, sure. 'Wow.' " He turned to me. "But that's the easy part," he said.

I had to speak up so he could hear me above the wind. "What's the hard part?"

"What comes next." He turned back to the sky. "Remember the first time we went out to dinner, how I said I used to go to the Point as a kid and look at the sky with my binoculars?"

"I remember."

"Well, as I kept looking, I kept learning more and more about the planets and stars and galaxies. And the more I learned, the more I wanted to know. So I'd keep going back there, and in time I started bringing star charts and then I started investing in better equipment. The more I'd find, the more I couldn't wait to get back there and try something even more difficult, and more, and more. It's funny," he said. "At first I brought those binoculars out there to try to find my mother, but then I used them to look at stars and planets. And as I did, I kind of stopped thinking about my mother so much. It's like I incorporated her into myself—what she'd meant to me. She always wanted me to go further and further. To push myself, like she'd done in her own life. To go as far as my mind or my legs or whatever could take me. This was something I got from her. And I never lost it."

I reached out to touch David's shoulder. I put my other hand on his chest, and I leaned into his arm, hard. He was looking up, and I was right there with him, looking up, too, and for the first time I felt I might be seeing what David was seeing.

"But the thing is," he went on, "the time comes when you begin to realize that the more you look, the less you know. For a while, sure, you understand how 'Wow' it all is. How far apart everything in the universe is. How absolutely lonely it is out there. And then it's too much, and you can't make sense of it. What's the difference between a billion years or ten billion years? Between a trillion miles and a hundred trillion miles?"

He stopped, once more considering whether to go on.

"But it's not just that," he said. "It's not just how big everything is, or how old. It's what happens out there." He laughed, but it was a bitter kind of laugh. "I'm sorry to say this, Liz, but the universe is not a happy place. It's full of unspeakable violence. You know those TV documentaries about animals in the wilderness, and everything looks so peaceful out there on the African veld? Or in your own backyard? But then you get closer, and you look closer, and all of a sudden things don't seem so calm. All of a sudden you see the way things really are, the way animals are always hunting one another and killing one another, and how they have to do that in order to survive. And you try to tell yourself, Nature is like that. And it is. But that doesn't mean you have to like it.

"Well, the universe is a lot like that, only a million times worse," he went on. "A billion times. It doesn't look it, does it? Not standing here, staring up at all those beautiful little lights. But it is. It's ruthless. It's full of things devouring one another, burning up and exploding and crashing into one another and then disappearing forever. Galaxies come to life, a hundred billion stars at a time, and a few billion years later the stars start to blink out, one by one, and then a few billion years later they're all gone. And once there was this beautiful spiral of light, with who knows how many stars with who knows how many planets and who knows how many civilizations, and then it's gone. Now you see it, now you don't."

"Fire and ice," I said, thinking of the meteor we'd seen together that first night at the Point.

"And how do you make sense of that?" he said. "Why do you even try? But you do. You try." He stopped. His head was up, staring down the heavens themselves. "That's the hard part," he finally said.

"To keep looking," I said.

He nodded. For once, I knew what to say. I knew exactly what to say. I just didn't know if I dared to say it. But I knew this, too: If I didn't say it, David and I would never have a chance.

"You can stop looking now," I said softly.

For a moment, David didn't respond. Then he said, "I know. That's what terrifies me the most."

As we stood there, I had to use the back of my hand to wipe the tears from my face, and then from his. Still, we didn't move. It was as if neither of us wanted to leave the mountain just yet. We stood there a few minutes longer, not just leaning into each other in the absolute darkness of the end of the world, but leaning into each other in the absolute darkness of the end of the world together.

*Chapter
Six*

∞ On our final afternoon in Hawaii, after we'd eaten one last meal at the hotel's seaside restaurant and gone for one last dip in the ocean, David announced he had an errand to run, something he needed to do alone. When he returned to our room a short while later he asked me to close my eyes and hold out my hand. I felt something light and square descend there, and when I opened my eyes I found that he'd presented me with a tiny box. It was wrapped in tissue paper the same shade as the sea outside our window, and it was small enough to hold a piece of jewelry—a ring, maybe.

"Oh," I said.

"Open it."

The truth was, I didn't know if I wanted to.

If it was a ring, something signifying an engagement, a proposal of marriage, then the gesture seemed premature, impetuous. Still, I couldn't very well refuse to open his gift. As I turned the box over and slipped a fingernail under the tape, I noticed that my hands were trembling slightly. The two halves of the turquoise tissue paper parted easily and fell to the carpet. I turned the box over, lifted the lid, separated tufts of cotton and saw, at the bottom of the box, a glimmer of gold. I reached inside and pinched my fingers around—

"A key?"

"To Stardust," David said, looking away from me, slightly embarrassed. "So that later on, after you go back to Longwood Falls, and you want to come down to Stone Point to visit, you can just let yourself in." He paused. "Look, Liz, I wouldn't presume to ask you to give up your life in Longwood Falls," he said. "Your house, your job, your friends. It wouldn't be fair. And I can't leave my students. But I guess I'm secretly hoping you'll start to think of the observatory as a kind of second home. A place you can come to whenever you want."

"Are you sure?" I asked.

"Yes," he said. "Completely. I just know that I want us to be together as much as possible, in whatever way we can." He stopped and gave me an odd look. "Are *you* sure?"

It was strange: Although I'd been involved with a few different men over the years, no one had ever given me his key, and no one had ever been given mine. Even that lawyer Jeff Hardesty, with whom I'd been serious, had never been someone I really wanted to come home to.

But with David, I could imagine letting myself into that place where I felt so comfortable, that place where I knew he waited. Now I came forward and kissed him, my fingers closing hard over the golden key.

The following afternoon, after a disorienting night of air travel, David and I leaning against each other and sleeping for brief periods of time, I was back at my sister's house. My arms were heavy with gifts for Nick: three different kinds of macadamia nuts, a puzzle in the shape of Hawaii, a make-your-own-volcano kit, and, of course, one rock. The taxi from the airport had dropped a sleepy, stumbling David off at the observatory, then took me on to The Eaves, but when I walked in the front door, I was met with a surprise.

Harper was standing there.

For a second I just stared, as though she was just a mirage caused by extreme jet lag.

"Aren't you going to say hello?" my sister asked me, and in a shaky voice I dutifully said hello, put down my bags, then came forward and kissed her.

"What are you doing here?" I asked.

"I thought I would surprise you," Harper said. "I was getting kind of antsy down there on the island, and I missed Nick so much, and I just thought to myself: It's time. So yesterday I decided I'd arrange for my return to coincide with yours. I took a flight out of Florida at the crack of dawn. And here I am."

There she was. She looked better; I could see that right away. Her hair was growing back, turning stylish again, her skin was tan, and she no longer wore the intensely shell-shocked look she'd worn the day of the funeral. Harper seemed more rested now, though the area around her eyes still looked raw from crying and rubbing. It had been difficult to tell how she was doing from our brief and awkward phone conversations during her time in Florida, but now I could see that she was, if nothing else, intact.

Before I had a chance to say anything else to her, though, Nick bounded down the stairs to see me. He looked different too, maybe simply because he was running in the house; but it was almost as though in my short time away he'd actually changed in some physical way. Then I realized that if he looked different at all it wasn't because I had been gone. It was because his mother was back.

The three of us went and sat in the family room, and Nick opened his presents on the floor. As he put together the volcano, Harper turned to me and quietly said, "I want to thank you, Liz. You took good care of Nick."

"I loved it," I said. "He's a wonderful boy. We've really gotten to know each other."

"Well," she said, "you've still got to be pretty tired of being a baby-sitter. Now that I'm back, you're relieved of your duties. You can go back to your own life." I didn't say anything. "I thought you'd be glad," she said. But when I looked at her with a complicated expression apparent on my face, Harper said, "Oh." Then she nodded her head lightly. "It's David," she said. "Of course. I should have realized."

And she was right; it was David. I hadn't expected Harper back quite so soon, and her presence here in the house left me free to go back to my old life. Yet suddenly, faced with that option, it seemed far from desirable, and even before I knew what I was saying, I'd said it, and I'd meant it:

"Actually—actually, I'm not going back."

Later that afternoon, I stopped by the observatory to tell David what I wanted to do. He blinked several times, absorbing the news, then kissed me hard and lifted me high in the air. I made him swear that if he had any reservations about my staying on in Stone Point he had to tell me right now, but he promised that he had none.

"Are you kidding?" he said. "This is what I was hoping you'd decide to do."

"You should have said something," I said.

"You could have said something, too," David answered, and I laughed lightly.

"Well," I said, "now I have."

"Okay," he said. "Now it's my turn to say something." He leaned into me and whispered. "Let's go to bed."

I laughed again. "I have to get back to

The Eaves for dinner," I said. "I promised Nick and Harper."

"Dinner's not for a couple of hours."

I glanced over at the bed, and I imagined slipping under that Mexican comforter with David, our bodies lightly touching, and that first touch turning to desire, and that desire turning to need. "Well, maybe I could stay for a little while," I said.

This was new to me—this kind of impetuousness, this throwing of caution to the wind. I had to ask myself if it was simply the abruptness of Harper's return, the prospect of suddenly saying good-bye to Nick and David, that made me decide to stay in Stone Point. But no; instead, Harper's surprise reappearance at The Eaves simply set into relief what I really felt. David and I had spoken of the future in vague, sketchy terms. We knew we wanted to continue to be involved after I went back to Longwood Falls, and now I even had a key to the observatory. We'd spoken casually of a long-distance re-

lationship. But in truth, neither of us felt remotely casual about the other person.

The logistics of this new life would have to
be worked out, of course. I would have to
sell my house, leave my job, make a clean
break from the life I'd been fastened into for
so long. I had no idea if I would be able to
get a job at the Stone Point Library; if not,
there were other libraries in nearby towns,
but finding a job would take some doing.
And would I actually live with David, or perhaps find my own apartment in Stone Point
and live there until we were really sure?
Still, after making love, as we lay together
on David's bed and the last streaks of twilight left the sky outside the window and
neither of us made a move to turn on a light,
it was possible to imagine that many days
might end like this for years to come.

In the past, when I was involved with
someone I'd find myself looking forward to
our time together; but then after a while I
would also find myself looking forward to

my time alone. That wasn't the case here. In our short time together David and I had already fallen into a rhythm as if we'd been doing this all our lives, because, in a way, we had. One week we were living apart and alone, following our predictable individual paths through the emptiness of space; the next, we'd fallen into each other's orbits, there to follow the graceful tug and pull of our mutual attraction.

"Better be careful," David said to me in bed, when I tried out for him this astronomical interpretation of our lives. "We don't want to *collide*, or anything."

"Oh, I don't know. I've got no complaints about the collision we just had."

He smiled. "I mean the crash-and-burn kind."

"So do I."

This was new for me, too: Never had I felt so free with another man. In my experience, intimate references had always been furtive or secretive. Now I understood that there was an alternative. Right from the start David and I had exhibited an ease with each other in every way, a physical knowingness that, afterward, translated into casual talk. I could remember rising from Jeff's bed and looking back to see the same four-cornered formality that had been there half an hour earlier. But a bed I shared with David always ended up in a sweep of sheets like shifting sands, a landscape crafted by natural forces.

Yet in one important way, it seemed to me, David couldn't be romantic. As loving as he could be with me, he could be unsparing when it came to his other love, the night sky. Yes, I had learned to look at the heavens the way David did—to see in the stars the same unforgiving character that a man who'd lost his mother as a little boy might find there. But couldn't he learn to see what I saw above, too: light, beauty, hope?

"David," I said, "aren't there any double planets or stars or whatever out there that *don't* crash and burn? Is that what you tell your students the heavens are all about—doom and gloom?"

A full moon was just rising above the stand of trees outside the window. David studied me closely in the bluish light that lay across our bed. "Okay," he finally said, and suddenly he got up on his knees, faced the window, and unlatched it. He pushed out, and winter air rushed in.

"What are you doing?"

"Just a minute," he said, and he leaned out the window. I got up on my knees and joined him. Side by side we kneeled there, elbows on the ledge, craning out into the cold evening air. He was straining to see something almost directly overhead.

I breathed deeply. I could smell the salt-water from the Sound.

"There we go," he said. "See Orion?"

I followed his gaze. "The three stars in a row right there?" I said.

"Now look a little bit above them, to the left. Those two bright stars?"

"I see them."

"Liz Mallory, I give you Castor and Pollux," he said. "Sons of Zeus. Twins, actually. Oh."

"What's the matter?"

"Nothing. I just realized, you know, *twins*. Like you and Harper."

"Well, that's all right," I said. I brought my head back through the window into the cottage. "No crashing and burning there," I said. "Not anymore."

The following afternoon I picked Nick up at school, pulling my car up to the end of the line of vehicles in the long driveway. This time I was early, and I got out of the car. I paced the sidewalk, going past the other women waiting outside their cars, and I strained for a glimpse of David's classroom through the windows of the school across the lawn.

I saw him at the far end of the second floor. Some sort of presentation seemed to be in progress. Through the tall, arched windows I could see a little girl holding a giant hand-painted picture of the Sun over her head while boys and girls holding pictures of planets circled around her. There was blue Earth, red Mars, giant Jupiter, ringed Saturn. *Our* Saturn, a role, I noticed, that David had given to Nick. And there at the head of the classroom, choreographing the dance of the solar system, was David, nodding his head and waving his arms in some grand explanation, and an odd thing happened then. It wasn't the eighteen or so kids in his classroom who I imagined him teaching at that moment; it was our own child, the boy or girl we might have together. The child I suddenly couldn't wait to meet, the child I suddenly couldn't bear to be without. Or children. Twins. After all, they ran in my family.

I stood as if in a trance, watching the planets make their revolution, watching life go on and on, endlessly and effortlessly, bringing love with it, and sadness, and children, and entire unexpected lives. It wasn't until David dismissed his students and they pulled off their costumes and began to stream from the classroom, that I finally stopped looking.

Afterward, when I drove Nick home to The Eaves and I was heading up the front steps, planning to stop inside the house just long enough to gather up my belongings to take over to David's, I caught sight of Harper coming up the path from the woods. She was wearing an old sweatshirt streaked with smears of yellow and blue, and suddenly I realized what she'd been doing.

"Harper, you've been painting," I said, walking back down the steps.

She shrugged, seeming self-conscious for a moment, as though she'd been caught doing something illicit. "Not really," she said. "Just mixing some colors. Experimenting a little." She lowered her eyes.

"Well, I'd love to see the studio sometime," I said. "When you're ready."

She stopped on the path, considering.

"I confess Nick and I looked through the window once while you were gone," I said. "It looked beautiful."

Harper looked back up at me, and then she gestured with her head and said, "Okay. Come on."

What she had said so rashly before heading down to Florida—that she would never paint again—wasn't true anymore. But in her manner my sister was also making it clear that she wasn't yet comfortable returning to her work, that she was on fragile ground here—or on *no* ground, as if she were on a tightrope. As we approached the clearing in the woods, I understood it was my responsibility not to say or do anything, as she was taking these first, tentative steps, that might make her look down.

The padlock on the studio was gone now, and the door swung open easily. My sister stepped aside, and I entered before her.

"It's a wonderful place," I said quietly.

"Yes," said Harper, as if, even after all these years, she were as much in awe of this safe haven she'd created for herself in the middle of the woods as a visitor might be. "It really is."

"When we were girls," I said, "you used to tell Mom and Dad that you were going to have a real studio someday when you were a real artist. Is this the way you pictured it?"

Harper paused, thinking about this, and then she nodded. "Yes," she said. "I think it is." After a moment she added, "But the rest of my life isn't. I'm not sure *what* I pictured."

She walked over to the cot in the corner of the room and sat down. I followed her and sat beside her. Our knees brushed against each other. "To answer your question from before," she said, "I mean, to answer it more truthfully, I *have* been painting a little. I started during my last few days on Sanibel Island. It was strange. I woke up one morning from a dream, and my hand was actually *moving*, as though it held a paintbrush. I guess painting comes so naturally to me that I do it in my sleep." She shook her head. "I've had an idea about a painting. Several ideas. A series of paintings, actually—" She stopped herself. "I don't really want to talk about it, though. It's too new, too raw." She looked down. After a moment, she looked up again, right into my eyes. "Nick says he really missed you when you went to Hawaii."

"I missed him."

My sister smiled slightly, to herself. "Do you know what he's made me promise I'll do tonight when you're gone? Play Clue with him. God, I can't remember the last time I played Clue."

"No, you never were big on board games, were you?" I said to her.

"I never had the patience for them. They bored me to tears. They still do."

"But you'll play Clue for Nick's sake," I said.

"Yes," she said. "It's what mothers do. I'm finding that out, finally. It's the little things, the things that seem so trivial—that's what children care about. The big stuff—the fact that you've given them a trust fund, or a beautiful home on the water—they barely notice. But if you sit down on the floor and play Clue with them, they're thrilled to pieces."

"Yes," I said. "They are."

There was a long pause, and I saw that Harper seemed to be struggling to say something. She reached out, and I allowed her to take my hands in hers, as if it were the most natural gesture in the world between the two of us. "Being with David," she finally said, "it seems to have done something for you. You seem different. Much more open. Less guarded. I feel like I can really talk to you for the first time." She paused uneasily. "Or maybe it's me that's changed."

"Harper—" I said.

"No, please. Let me finish." She was looking down at our joined hands. "I've been meaning to say this, but it's hard. It's always been hard. You'd think with the two of us being twins it would be easy to talk like this. But sometimes I think we had it harder than regular sisters."

"In a way, we did," I said.

She released my hands then. She let go and raised her arms, spreading them wide, as if to take in the studio, the estate, and all of Stone Point. "Can you believe this life I've fallen into?" She shook her head. "It's not what we knew in Longwood Falls, is it?"

"No, it's not."

"I know how it must seem to you, having Jeannette and Tom working for me, and all this space. But it's hard to keep it all straight in your head. Please believe me. It creeps up on you, like an addiction. It's like: Here's a little something that will make your life a little easier, and here's a little something else, and now try this, and this, and this. And, of course, you want your life to be easier, so you say yes to everything, but then one day you turn around and suddenly you're not the person you thought you were. The person you ever wanted to be." She took a breath. "Anyway, I just want to say that Nick thinks you're a terrific aunt. And I'm glad you're going to be living so nearby."

"It'll be good to be here," I said. "There, I mean." I waved vaguely. "Wherever."

My sister abruptly stood up from the cot.

"I've got to get out of these clothes," she said suddenly. "I must look like a walking Jackson Pollock painting. Would you excuse me for a second?"

"Sure," I said.

As Harper walked toward the bathroom to wash and change out of her paint-spattered clothing, I asked her if I could take a look around.

"Why not?" she said, shrugging, and then she went into the bathroom, shutting the door behind her. I was tempted to leave her then, to let myself out and not risk spoiling the fragile moment. It had been glorious to watch my sister start to come back, to slowly return from wherever it was she'd retreated this past month. To *more* than come back— to get outside of herself, to extend herself to me in a way she never had. And then it occurred to me that I had done exactly the same thing, with David.

I stood up and began to walk around the studio, really looking hard at the old canvases that leaned against walls, appreciating for the first time the detail of my sister's brushwork, and her use of complex color, hybrid tones that I'd never seen before. I walked over to a large wooden storage rack where she kept some of her finished paintings, and carefully I lifted one out from its slot. It was a beautiful, if melancholy, painting of Nick and Doe, done when they were small. They sat leaning together, exhausted, as if at the end of a very long day. After a moment I slipped the painting back in and took out the next one, which was a painting of Carlo, dressed in a pale linen summer suit, looking every bit as commanding and wealthy and elegant as he did in real life. My sister had a way of capturing the truth about people, a talent I could only admire.

I slipped the painting of Carlo back in its slot, and then I pulled out the next painting, lifting it swiftly. I stood holding it in both hands, and it took me only a moment to understand what I was looking at.

It was a painting of David, and in it he lay naked on a bed, sprawled with unmistakable ease across a Mexican comforter decorated with colorful zigzags.

*Chapter
Seven*

⚮ "Clean at last," called Harper from the bathroom.

I kept looking at the painting, not taking my eyes off it. David's body was fully visible: the long legs, the tapering of hair on the torso, the musculature, the entire beautiful body that I had touched and held, and which, in some way, I had almost begun to feel belonged to me. David's eyes looked out at the person looking in, establishing an intimate connection. From the depths of the canvas, he was speaking to me. He was telling me something that I suppose I should have always known, something that I should have been able to guess. For why else had David lain in the bed in the observatory and let Harper paint him naked, why else had he smiled that lover's half smile at my sister as she put brush to canvas?

"Do you need more time to look around?" Harper called. I turned dully toward her voice. She walked back into the room tugging a comb through her hair with the same impatient gesture I'd watched since childhood. "Of course, the studio has seen better days." Her mouth was moving, making words, but I couldn't hear what she was saying. Instead, I just kept looking at that mouth, imagining it on David's. I imagined Harper putting down her paintbrush and joining David in his bed, our bed, the bed I now held in my hand.

I shoved the painting back in its slot.

"All set, Liz?"

I didn't move. Harper seemed to be waiting for some kind of response.

"Liz?" she said. "What's wrong?"

But I just stood there, not knowing where to look: not at Harper, not at the paintings, not at anything.

"Liz?"

The Observatory

Had he taken Harper upstairs to the observatory, too? Were all of the things he and I had experienced together things he'd experienced first with her? Was that what I'd been for David, what I'd always been throughout my life, a poor substitute for my sister? The safe one who followed slowly and cautiously behind, while she forged ahead, burning her way through the world?

"Liz, are you all right?" Harper's voice was strained with worry now. "What's going on?"

Or, worse, was it just physical, what they'd had? What they still had? Were they still lovers? If they could keep their shared history a secret from me, who knew what else they might keep from me. Suddenly, anything was possible.

"Liz—"

She was moving toward me. I turned away. I didn't want to see her face, feel her touch, be in the same room with her, the same house, the same town. But what choice did I have? I couldn't *not* be here. I had to find out. I had to know everything.

I lifted the painting again and turned it around so she could see it. And in that split second, looking at Harper's face, I had my answer. For her eyes had widened and her mouth had gone slack, and she had the unmistakable look of someone who has been caught.

"It's true, then," I began. She didn't reply. "You and David were lovers," I said.

She eased the painting from my hand and slowly returned it to where it had come from. "Yes," she said after a moment. "We were."

"Are you still?"

She looked up and shook her head vehemently. "No," she said. "Of course not. It ended two years ago." She waited a beat. "I wouldn't do that to you, Liz."

This comment enraged me. "You wouldn't do that," I said, "but instead you *would* keep this fact from me, as though it's completely irrelevant?"

"Let me explain—"

"You'd let me think that I was the one he

wanted," I interrupted, "when all along he was probably still thinking about you: the more dynamic twin, the more exciting one."

"Oh, I don't think so," she said.

"Come on, Harper," I went on. "They always think about you; they always get obsessed with you. I've seen it happen throughout our lives. Don't tell me you don't know what I'm talking about."

"I see. That's what this is really about, isn't it?" she said. "Look, I'm sorry now that I kept it from you, and I probably shouldn't have, but if this is just one more chance for you to feel sorry for yourself—"

"So why *didn't* you tell me?" I cut her off. "On the phone when I called you to ask about going to Hawaii? Or yesterday? Or today? What about five minutes ago, when we were sitting together on that cot over there and you were saying how you'd never been able to talk to me like this before?"

"Because it's *over*," she said. "There's nothing to tell about David and me."

"Nothing to tell? You call having had an

affair with the man your sister is seriously involved with 'nothing to tell'? My God, you have a warped view of life. You're right, Harper. This place, this life of yours, it really has done something to you."

"I'll tell you what it hasn't done," she said, her voice suddenly hard and cruel. "It hasn't made me small and meek and self-pitying."

I thought of how many times I'd watched her be the center of attention, the one who drew everyone to her. She'd had so much in her life: wealth, fame, children, lovers. She'd even briefly had David. Suddenly I stepped forward and did something I still can't quite believe I did: I slapped her.

Harper cried out and put her own hand to her face. There was a shocked silence as we both took in what I'd just done. Then she lowered her hand. Her cheek was pink from the slap, but she seemed to wear it like a badge of honor.

"At least," she said, "when I feel sorry for myself and go off somewhere and collapse, I've got a damn good reason."

I turned away. "That's not fair," I said.

"No, it's not," said Harper. "So what? Since when is life fair? If it was fair, I'd still have my daughter, wouldn't I?" I could hear her breathe heavily, gathering herself. "I'll tell you what happened, if you want to know."

I didn't answer. She went on.

"We were lovers years ago. We met jogging on the beach, and one thing led to another. My marriage had failed. I was lonely, and so was he. It wasn't love or anything like that. It was a thing. That's all it was, a physical thing."

"This is supposed to make me feel better?" I asked.

"I'm not saying it should make you feel better. I'm just trying to get you to see that this isn't about *you*. This is about something that happened a while ago to the man you love and a woman who just happens to be your sister. I realized I was on the rebound from Carlo," she went on in a quieter voice. "I was in no position to be seriously involved with anyone, and I broke it off. I handled it badly. He was angry. Furious, actually. Begged me to change my mind, but I wouldn't." She shrugged. "Occasionally, after that, we'd run into each other in town, but we didn't speak. It wasn't until this year, when Nick was in his class, that we had any contact with each other. And that's the whole story."

I looked at her fully then, saw her standing there with her fresh clothes and her inflamed cheek that still bore a light imprint of my hand. The whole effect was somehow dramatic and compelling. Here it was, all over again, the story of our lives—the story of two sisters, one unpredictable and beautiful, the other one less so. And in this story, the beautiful sister gets everything she wants, and the lesser sister gets whatever's left, and nothing Harper could say could change that.

"I have to go," I said.

"Liz, please."

"Is there anything else to say?" I asked. "Do you have something new to tell me?"

She shook her head.

"Then good-bye, Harper," I said, and I walked out of her studio. She knew where I was going, and she didn't try to follow.

On the drive to the observatory, I was buried in the images and thoughts that I already knew would be returning to me endlessly in the months and years to come: Harper and David in the observer's chair, rising toward the sky; Harper and David under the Mexican blanket on the bed in the cottage; Harper and David, separately, apart, going about their days, painting and teaching, conducting themselves in the world as all lovers do, with secrecy and excitement at the knowledge that soon they'd meet in a dim room, letting the rest of the world fall away.

As my car pulled up the driveway of Red Briar, passing the darkened, imposing house where Old Man Boyd was most likely fast asleep, and then approaching the observatory cottage, I could see that David's lights were still on. He heard my car and came to the door, his face breaking into a smile at my arrival. As recently as the day before, this had been a place I loved. *Stardust*. The low bed, the butcher-block kitchen table, the shelves crammed with astronomy books, the observatory overhead: All of it had felt like home, even before I'd had a chance to live there.

Now I stood looking past David and across the room, feeling a surprising sense of indifference toward the place, as though I'd never been here before. He saw something in my face and said to me, "Liz, what is it?"

I looked at him. "You and Harper," I said. "I know about the two of you."

He didn't reply but just stood there, shaken and unblinking.

"Were you planning on keeping it from me forever?" I asked.

David still appeared shocked, but finally he ran a hand through his tangle of hair and in a quiet voice he said, "No. No, I wasn't."

"You should have told me right away," I said.

"Why?" asked David.

"It was your responsibility."

"Who says?" he asked. "Why was it my responsibility to let you see how I was used by your sister? Why was it my responsibility to make myself look really pathetic in your eyes—to be just another jerk who got dumped by your sister?" He took a breath and stepped closer to me. "She used me, Liz. I was just this schoolteacher, and she was this big famous artist, and okay, we had an affair. I thought it was something more than that, but apparently I was way off." His face had high color in it as he spoke. "I didn't tell you at first because I was *embarrassed.* I just wanted the whole thing to be buried forever."

"Well, it's been dug up," I said. Something

occurred to me then. "She was the one who abandoned you, wasn't she?" I asked. "The woman you sometimes refer to."

"Yes," he said. "She was."

David paced around the cottage nervously, making a circle and then returning to me. "I was going to tell you eventually," he said. "Out of fairness to you. But I dreaded it, not only because I was humiliated, but also because I knew you'd be upset. You'd start assuming things that weren't true. You'd assume Harper was the real thing for me, and you were the consolation prize."

"That's exactly right," I said.

"Well, there you go," he said. "You have this idea, Liz, about you and your sister, whether or not it has anything to do with the truth."

"It *is* the truth," I said. "I think you got involved with me because I was the next best thing to her." I shook my head slightly, then added, "I don't want to be the next best thing."

"It's not a contest!" he said, and he was

shouting now. "For God's sake, can't you get that through your head? This isn't about you and your sister; it's about you and me!"

I looked away from him and around the small living room. I'd imagined growing older with David here, moving through our lives in moments of quiet and moments of noise, the way couples did. I saw us upstairs in the observatory, our future son or daughter sitting in David's lap as we went for a ride in the telescope's miraculously rising chair. Then the image began to fade, to disappear before it had had a chance to become real.

"I'm going home," I said to him.

"I'll come by tomorrow," David said quickly. "We can get past this."

"I mean *home*," I said. "I'm going home to Longwood Falls."

David stared at me. "Come on, Liz. You can do better than that."

"Apparently not." I turned to go.

"I suppose I should have expected this," he said.

I stopped.

"I've spent my whole life being extremely cautious, holding myself back." There was a sharp edge to David's voice that hadn't been there a moment before. He was rising to my level, rapidly becoming as angry as I was. "People *leave;* it's just what they do. Every single one of them does it, and you can tell yourself that you've found the exception, the one who's there for the long run, but you're only kidding yourself. I've seen the way people just walk out; I've seen it in action my entire life. But somehow I convinced myself that you were going to be different. That you would never do this to me." David shook his head. "But you're no different from any of them," he said. Then he took a sharp inward breath, and added, "You're no better than your sister. In some ways, maybe you're even worse. With you, there's this whole 'sweetness and light' thing. Small-town values. Runs a library. Cares about books. Takes good care of her nephew. A decent, thoughtful person who claims she wants a bigger life, something she can call her own. So then she's actually about to get that life, and what does she do? She lets it be destroyed by something that happened a long time ago. Something that's totally over."

I looked at David, not even trying to argue with what he was saying. The fact was, I'd always wonder whether he still quietly longed for Harper. I'd always feel like I was the one he settled for. There would always be a doubt in my mind, and I could never let it go. The idea of "getting past this"—of staying in Stone Point, of trying to establish a relationship with my sister and nephew while building a life with David—suddenly seemed absurd.

"I'm sorry," I whispered, barely able to find a voice.

He studied me for a moment. "Me, too," he said.

These were the last words David spoke to me before I left. I knew that they were likely to be the last words he would ever speak to me. The idea of never seeing him again, never hearing his voice, or waking up against him, our bodies slowly breaking the surface of sleep like two drowsy swimmers, left me breathless, stunned.

Now I silently said good-bye. David and I stood and looked at each other, and there was no way to undo this, to come gratefully into each other's arms as we'd done so many other nights in this cottage. Without another word I walked out, heading back to my car. Then something made me turn and look back. In one of the windows David suddenly appeared for a moment, and our eyes met, and then he stepped out of the frame for the very last time.

I needed to go back to Harper's house briefly to gather my small collection of belongings. I'd hoped to do it swiftly and quietly, not wanting to make a scene. But as I stood in the guest room packing, there was a knock on my door. I opened it, expecting that it was Harper.

But it was Nick. He was ready for bed, wearing his pajamas with the airplanes on them, and a pair of furry slippers in the shape of reindeer. His hair was still damp from his bath, and he was just standing there. It broke my heart to see him, to know what my unexpected departure was likely to do to him.

"Aunt Liz," he said. "I know it's late, but do you want to play something?" I shook my head no. "I've got this new board game where someone steals the crown jewels and you have to try and get them back. It's really cool."

"I'm so sorry, honey," I said quietly, and the phrase encompassed all that I felt for Nick in this moment.

He looked beyond me into the room, where my bag was open on the bed and some folded clothes lay beside it, about to be packed. "Are you getting ready to go to Mr. Fields's place?" he asked. I shook my head. "Then are you going somewhere else?" he went on. "Because maybe you could take me with you. I'm a very good traveler, did you know that? I never get sick in cars or airplanes," he said proudly.

"I can't take you with me, Nick," I said softly. I sighed heavily and came forward, taking his hands in mine, stooping down to look him in the eye. He gave off the innocent apple scent of some children's shampoo. "I'm leaving for real," I told him. "I'm going back to Longwood Falls."

He stared at me. "Longwood Falls?" he said. "You're going there? I thought you decided you weren't going to live there anymore. You said you weren't. When you came back from Hawaii you said you were going to stay here in Stone Point after all. That you'd still pick me up at school sometimes, and that we'd always do stuff."

"We can still do stuff," I said carefully, and my throat thickened; if I wasn't careful, I might start to cry, and I didn't want to do that right now. There had been enough pain in this house to last a lifetime. "You'll come and visit me," I said. "We'll arrange it as often as we can. I'm glad you don't get sick in cars." I was babbling now, but I had to try and keep this conversation from dissolving into tears.

"But you said—"

"Well, I changed my mind," I said. "As it turns out, I have to go back there after all."

"Forever?" he asked, and the word was chilling. *Was* this forever? Most likely, I knew, it was. People's lives didn't keep offering an unlimited series of new possibilities. As you got older, the options came fewer and farther between. For a brief moment there, I'd been willing to step out of that old life as though it were a dress that no longer looked right on me, and to try on something entirely new. A life that would fit me better, that I could wear for a long, long time.

"Yes," I said, nodding. "Probably forever."

Nick looked away from me, shifting his gaze toward the wall of windows and the Sound invisibly beyond. "I can't believe it," he said, his voice cracking.

"No, no, Nick, you'll be okay," I said gently. "You've got your mom back."

Nick turned back to me now, and something wild and fearful had entered his eyes. "You promised," he said, his voice rising up. "You *promised*." And with that he turned and ran from the room, bounding down the marble staircase. I heard the heavy front door of the house slam behind him.

"Nick!" I called, going after him, but by the time I made my way outside he had gone off somewhere into the dark. I wasn't sure which way he had run, and I was worried, for he was wearing only his airplane pajamas and reindeer slippers, and there was still snow on the ground. "Nick, wait!" I shouted, but there was no answer, and I couldn't hear his footsteps.

I turned back inside the house and ran upstairs. When I knocked on Harper's door and she called to me to come in, her silver hairbrush in hand, her hair still flyaway from the friction of the brush, I immediately told her what had happened, the words coming out all at once. Her eyes narrowed, and she laid the hairbrush down on the dressing table next to the door.

"What have you done?" Harper said, turning to me.

"I'm sorry," I tried. "It just happened, and—"

"I don't want to hear it," she said. She shrugged into her coat. "If anything happens to him . . . ," she said, letting her voice trail off. She'd already lost one child; now her second one was out there in the night. I followed her downstairs and stood on the front porch, watching as she ran frantically into the road, shouting Nick's name. But there was no answer; just the sound of her voice and the rolling shush of the water. My sister came back inside and pressed two call buttons on the house intercom, gathering Tom and Jeannette together. She handed out flashlights, and soon we were all off searching for Nick.

If anything happened to him, I knew I could never forgive myself. I suppose that I could have predicted he'd react very badly to my sudden departure, but when he showed up at the door of my room I hadn't been thinking about him at all. I'd only been thinking about myself and how I'd lost David even before we'd really had a chance to start our life together.

Now I grabbed the last flashlight. It was a sturdy, industrial light made out of silver metal, and it cast a broad beam. As I walked along the grounds of The Eaves, I swept the beam across trees and sky and the patchy snow that lined the ground. I headed down the path to my sister's art studio, thinking that perhaps Nick was hiding out there. But the place was completely dark. And then I realized where I'd find him.

As I came to the top of the hill where his sister had died, I stopped a moment and swept my flashlight across the open field. It took me only a moment to locate a tiny figure standing in the distance, just as I'd found him that first day, the afternoon of

Doe's funeral. When my flashlight hit him, he started to run.

"Nick!" I called, running down the hill after him.

"Go away," he said, just as he'd said that first day, but I caught up to him and grabbed a shoulder of his pajamas and held on. He slipped and fell to one knee, and then I slipped after him, and together we tumbled to the snow and dirt. "Get away from me!" he yelled, trying to stand up as I struggled to keep my grip on him. I wrapped him in my arms, smothering him like a fire with a blanket. "Let me go! Let me go!" His fists and legs were beating at me, catching me in the face and arms and chest. "I hate you!" he yelled. "Let me go! Mommy! Mommy! Mommy!"

And then a hand was on my shoulder, a firm, adult grip, pulling me back. I looked up to find Tom, the butler, standing over us.

"That's enough now," Tom said, and Nick grew still.

And then Harper caught up to us and reached past me to Nick, kneeling down and gathering her son tightly in her arms, wrapping him up in them as though she would never let go. I stayed sitting on the damp, cold earth, trying to catch my breath while the two of them leaned into each other, crying and sobbing together.

"I miss Doe," I heard Nick say. "Oh, Mommy, I miss her so much."

"So do I," Harper said.

"I can't believe it," he said. "I'll never see her again. Never!"

"I can't believe it either," said Harper.

"Oh, Mommy."

"Nick, sweetie, oh, my Nick."

"She was laughing so much. Remember how she laughed sometimes, and it sounded almost like a scream? When she went down the hill she was just laughing and laughing like that."

"I know."

"It's not fair."

"No. No, it's not. Not fair at all."

"I'm worried that I'll forget her, Mommy. Because sometimes I forget things. Last week I forgot my homework."

"Oh, no, Nick, we won't forget her. Not ever."

I'd caught my breath now. I stood up and backed away, until I couldn't hear what they were saying anymore, until I couldn't even tell whether they were talking or just rocking each other in the moonlight, swaying slightly, taking comfort and giving it back in whatever way they could. It was difficult now to tell who was holding on to whom.

Tom and Jeannette had closed around them. I was standing outside their circle now, watching from several paces back. I thought how different Harper seemed from the woman who had lain in her bed the day of Doe's funeral, unconcerned that Nick was outside alone in a snowstorm. She was upset now, she was frightened, but one thing was certain: Harper had come back to life. It was strange the way this worked, I thought. Bad things sometimes brought good, almost in afterthought.

And good things brought bad. I had let myself fall in love for the first time ever, and look what had happened. But I couldn't think about David anymore tonight. I was tired, and it was late, and I had a very long drive ahead of me. I was thirty-six years old, and for the briefest of moments I'd let myself be opened like the aperture of one of David's telescopes, finally letting in light.

Chapter
Eight

∞ So I did what I knew how to do best: I fled. I drove long into the night, stopping at 2 A.M. for coffee and a slice of cold pie at one of those roadside rest stops. The place was gloomy and fluorescent, and the only other people there were a couple of truck drivers on a break, and a few solo drivers like myself who were trying to keep themselves alert with an infusion of sugar and caffeine. Everyone in that rest stop—sitting alone at their booths, or on the swivel stools at the counter hunched over their own steaming coffee and plates of pie—was alone. I was just one more solitary person on the road in the middle of the night. This was the way I'd been before I'd come to Stone Point, and this was the way I'd left.

I couldn't bear to sit there too long, among these people who seemed to define the lonely life. Perhaps some of them had families to go home to, husbands or wives keeping the bed warm, smiling sleepily as they heard the key in the lock in the early hours of the morning. Maybe some of them had children, who would jump on their parents the minute they walked in the door, and frisk them for presents. But certainly at least a few of them were as alone as I was now, and would be going home to an empty house. I left some dollar bills on the table and went back to my car, and then I drove the rest of the way without stopping.

Throughout the ride, I kept picturing David, remembering how it had felt to be held by him, to lie against him all night and to keep looking at him, feeling as though I could have spent a lifetime examining the planes of his chest, the hair that fanned out along those planes, and everything else that made up who he was: his history, the things he loved, the things that scared him. Everything else about him that had felt, for a while, as though it was mine to explore.

By the time I left the highway at the exit marked LONGWOOD FALLS, and pulled into the driveway of my house, the sky was still black. I turned the key in the ignition, and the car quieted. I looked out the window; there was my house, an inanimate object waiting in the dark. I hadn't been inside in a very long time. Soon I would be turning on the lights, running my finger along the surfaces of tables to feel the light feathering of dust that would need to be gotten rid of tomorrow. Soon I would be reacquainting myself with all the things that I'd been willing to abandon. Soon I'd be returning to what I'd once been.

I stepped out of the car, walked up the steps onto the porch, and opened my screen door, hearing the familiar, rusty squeak that I'd never gotten around to fixing. All it needed was a drop of oil; I'd go to Handy Al's Hardware and take care of that tomorrow. Al himself, a soft-spoken old guy who'd

owned that store since I was a little girl,
would ask me how I'd been, say he hadn't
seen me lately, and I'd tell him I'd been out
of town for a while, but I was home for good.

Now I opened the front door, stepping into
the cold house and immediately reaching for
the light switch on the left wall. The front
hall brightened, revealing my home exactly
the way I'd left it, though somehow sadder,
smaller. The white gauzy curtains, the sofa
with its paisley pattern, the throw pillows
everywhere. It was a pretty house, certainly,
and ample in size, and yet it was clearly the
house of one person, not two. There were no
casual touches that meant another person
lived here. No worn leather men's gloves lay
on the front hall table, no men's running
shoes were on the mat. There were no romantic photographs scattered around of a
man and woman together in various locales.

I put my keys and pocketbook down on
the front table and went to the thermostat,
turning the knob until I heard the heat click
on and begin to whir into activity some-

where behind the walls. For a while there, I thought as the house warmed and I walked through the rooms, checking things, I had borrowed David, taken pleasure from his beautiful eyes and hands and mouth and the sadness that was as much a part of him as the features on his face.

Harper had once borrowed David for a while, too, had admired all the things about him that I'd admired. And he had admired her as well. There was no fooling myself. I was the less worldly sister, the less polished one. I looked back on the time I had spent with David, and suddenly I was embarrassed. What had he really thought of me? I wondered, but I had no way of ever finding out.

So here I was, back in Longwood Falls in the middle of the night. I went upstairs now to my bedroom. The blue spread was still smoothly stretched out on the bed the way I had left it when I'd hastily headed off to Doe's funeral. I took off my clothes now and bunched them up into a ball, which I tossed

onto a chair. Then I climbed into bed without a nightgown, wanting to feel the puni-
tively cold sheets against my skin. I shut off
the little lamp on my bedside table and lay
in the blank darkness for a while, telling
myself that I was home again, but knowing
that it wasn't really true.

As the weeks passed, I found myself slowly
returning to my old routine, and I tried very
hard to convince myself that I was the same
person I'd been when I'd lived here before.
But I couldn't fool myself into thinking that
was so, and in fact I couldn't even fool any of
my friends at the library. Several people
commented that I seemed "different."

One day, as I stood at the copy machine at
work, making copies of some document, my
friend Ellen, the harried reference librarian,
confronted me and said that she was worried. "About what?" I asked mildly.

"About you," she said. "You're totally different, Liz. I almost feel as though you've
had a complete personality change. Is there

anything you want to talk about? Anything I could help you with?"

I fed the machine another piece of paper, and shook my head no. So it was impossible to keep the changes in me from being seen. They were too profound, too extreme. I'd gone to Stone Point quietly lonely and passive, but I'd returned with an air of heartbreak that couldn't be disguised.

Then, one Saturday afternoon in late March, a library intern came into my office and told me that a man was here to see me. "He didn't give his name," the intern said. I stood quickly, my throat suddenly going dry. If it was David out there, what would I say to him? How would I react? I smoothed down my blouse and quickly raked a hand through my hair, and walked out of my office.

But there, standing by the circulation desk, was a man who bore no resemblance to David Fields. It was Jeff Hardesty, the lawyer with whom I'd been involved years earlier, before our relationship dwindled and he moved up to Buffalo. He looked slightly older now, of course, and his blond hair had thinned, but he was essentially the same, a pleasant if ordinary-looking man in a gray business suit.

When Jeff saw me, he smiled and kissed my cheek, and told me how glad he was to see me. It seemed that he had just moved back to Longwood Falls, where he was going to be joining the town's oldest law firm. The Victorian house he had bought was six blocks away from mine. "Would you have a drink with me later, Liz?" he asked.

I paused, considering, but realized I wasn't quite up to it. "I'm kind of busy, Jeff," I told him, and he said that it was all right, he'd be back. He looked at me with an extended gaze, and I knew he was trying to see whether there was anything there, anything left between us that hadn't completely disappeared over time. I turned away uneasily. It wasn't just that I felt Jeff and I had taken our relationship as far as it could go. It was also that I still felt myself to be emotionally unavailable, that in some way I thought

I still belonged to David, even though we hadn't seen each other for many weeks. I was still lost in a kind of sadness, a melancholy meditation on what I'd given up, and it threatened to take me over competely.

Everyone saw how unhappy I was, not just my friends and coworkers, but also Aunt Leatrice, who even at her age never missed a trick. When I first came back to Longwood Falls, she was, of course, very pleased to have me back, but still she admitted to being puzzled by why I'd left Stone Point on such obviously bad terms with Harper.

"You're sisters, you two," she said when I came and visited her for tea one afternoon. "I just don't understand what's happening. Please tell me."

I shook my head, declining to offer an explanation.

"Well," she said, "both of you are being extremely mysterious." She reached into the pocket of her sweater and slowly withdrew a folded piece of paper, which she handed to me without a word. Puzzled, I took it from her, seeing that Harper's raised initials were engraved in maroon on cream stationery.

"I received this yesterday," said Aunt Leatrice.

So here was the reason that I'd been invited to tea this afternoon—to read the letter from Harper. I opened the note warily and began to read:

Dear Aunt Leatrice,

I was so glad to hear from you last week and have that good talk. I understand how you feel about the situation with Liz, and I respect your point of view, but I also want to ask that you trust me in terms of how I am handling things. You tell me that my grief has clouded my perceptions, but I have to disagree. If anything, the grief that I've experienced this year has made me more able than ever to see things as I've never seen them before. And this is what I see:

That I wasn't a terrific sister. I know

that siblings often have problems, but I think they were particularly extreme in our case.

That I wasn't a terrific mother. As you know, Liz came and stayed after the accident, and basically took over all the responsibilities for Nick while I was hiding out in Florida. Of course, he's seven years old and it's not as though he wears diapers that need changing, but I suppose that before she arrived I never understood exactly what Nick did need. And now I do. He and I are close in a way that we never were before. Our lives have a terrible, shared emptiness in them since Doe died. But they also seem to have an emptiness—a surprising one—since Liz left.

I don't really want to go into details about the rift between Liz and me. Let's just say that I withheld information from her, so she's withholding herself from me.

I guess I'll sign off now, Aunt Leatrice. I am working on a new series of paintings, and I'd love for you to see them sometime.

Love,
Harper

P.S. Nick would like to add a few words.

At the bottom of the letter were several sentences in Nick's large handwriting. He printed his words in neat, square letters, having not learned script yet. Nick wrote:

Dear Aunt Leatrice,

How are you? I am fine. My mother bought me an iguana. I named him Seymour.

Love,
Your great-nephew Nick

P.S. And I really am "great"!

I smiled at Nick's words and handed the letter back to my aunt, who sat watching me expectantly. I'd written to Nick several times, but he'd never responded. Seeing his simple handwriting now made me long to be with him.

"Well?" Aunt Leatrice asked.

"Well what?" I said. "I'm not sure exactly what you want me to say."

But even though I didn't want my aunt to see it, I was feeling a great deal in that moment. As I read Harper's words, I had more of an understanding of the person behind them. And reading Nick's brief note at the bottom made me long to see him, to return to my role as his aunt and his friend, even though he wanted nothing to do with me.

"Liz, I'm a silly old lady," said Aunt Leatrice. "And I know that silly old ladies usually aren't taken seriously when they speak, but I want you to listen to me." I looked at my aunt. She blotted her lips with a napkin. "It's never easy being someone's sister," she said. "Your own mother and I— we had a hard time of it."

"You did?" I said. It was the first I'd ever heard of this.

"Oh, yes," she said, and her expression was one of someone who is remembering things that happened long ago. "Your mother could be quite difficult," she went on. "Of course, we weren't twins, and we didn't have to share a room, but there was always a certain kind of competition between us. An antagonism. I'm not sure how it started, but I think it worked both ways."

I was very surprised to hear all this. In my memories, my mother was easygoing, temperate, extremely fair. She'd always tried to encourage a friendship between Harper and me, and it had troubled her that no natural affection ever seemed to develop between her daughters. But I'd never taken her for someone who would give her own sister a hard time. "You were so close as adults," I said. "How did you get to that point?"

My aunt shrugged. "I don't know exactly," she said. "It was just one of those things. I guess we were able to let go of the past, let go of all the hurt and anger that had built up over the decades. All I know is that one day it was gone, and she and I were friends. We stayed that way until the day she died."

But I wasn't like my aunt; I couldn't let go of the fact that Harper had betrayed me, or, for that matter, that David had. I guess I was more stubborn than the other women in the family. "Harper and I can't be friends," I said to my aunt.

She looked at me sternly, and then after a moment she sighed. "I'm very sorry to hear you say that, Liz," she said. Then she stood up extremely slowly, clutching the edge of the table to balance herself. "I need to take a rest now," she said, ending our visit, and I knew she was disappointed in me, in my failure to rise to the occasion. I helped Aunt Leatrice upstairs to her bedroom, then I left her house, heading out into the fading afternoon.

One Thursday night I held a meeting of the book group I ran at the library. The group had ceased meeting in my absence, and now everyone seemed grateful that I was back and that we could continue. The novel that one of the members had requested we read this week was a love story about a soldier who is killed in World War II, and the woman who is unable to forget him. As we all sat on the comfortable couches of the library lounge eating doughnuts, I read a passage aloud:

> *Eleanor would never stop thinking about Michael, no matter how many years passed. What she felt was what countless women had felt when they'd lost their men. The pain of it would suddenly rise up out of nowhere, blocking all houses, lights, signs of life. She would remember him forever, because memory was a way of holding on to someone when the arms could not.*

After I finished reading the passage, the women sat in silence for a moment. There was a tension in the air, and I'm sure almost everyone was thinking about a specific person they'd once loved, and who was gone. But my own experience of love and loss was too fresh, too recent, and I found it intolerable to sit there, so I excused myself from the room for a moment.

"Are you all right?" a kind, motherly older woman named Valerie asked me as I stood, and I told her I was fine, and shakily left the room.

As I went, the women were murmuring behind me, and I heard one of them say, "Since she's been back, she seems different, doesn't she?"

I was going to have to get a grip on myself; I couldn't go on like this. I ended the book group a little earlier than usual that night, and then went for a drive through town by myself. With spring arriving, Longwood Falls was a pretty place, almost a place of perfection. The town was landlocked, but as a girl I'd never felt restless or imprisoned here the way that Harper had. Instead, I'd had a feeling of security, because I knew every inch of

Longwood Falls—its fields and walkways, the gazebo in the town square—and knew that there were very few surprises to be found. It was only since I'd left David that Longwood Falls seemed to me to be enclosing me against my will.

Now I went home again to my empty house, tossing my keys lightly on the hall table and heading into the kitchen. I noticed that the light on the answering machine was blinking, and I went to play back the messages. I was barely listening, when suddenly the kitchen was filled with a familiar voice. David's voice. My breath caught.

"Hi, Liz," he said quietly, hesitantly. "Are you there?" he asked, and then he patiently waited to see whether I was screening calls and would pick up the telephone. "I suppose you're not," he went on after a few seconds. "Look, I recently came across the roll of film we took in Hawaii. I guess I forgot all about it, and so I brought it in to the drugstore and today the pictures came back." He paused. "God, you look so pretty in them,"

226

he said. "That trip was wonderful, wasn't it?" He got silent again, and then he said, "I think it's crazy that we're not speaking. There's a lot that I want to say. You didn't give me the chance the night you left. So please," he said, "give me a call when you get home." He paused, and then he added, "I miss you." There was a thud and a click as David hung up his phone.

I felt light-headed, and carefully sat down at the kitchen table. I missed him so much, too, but when I considered picking up the phone and actually calling him, I remembered the painting in Harper's studio, and how badly I'd felt David had treated me. I was aware that I'd treated him badly, too, but I didn't know how else to behave, and so I didn't call him.

Two days later David called me again, but now I was in fact screening my calls, and I forced myself not to pick up. He called again one more time after that, and still I didn't take the call. And then he never called again.

I was agitated constantly as the weeks passed and could barely sleep. Whenever I did sleep I dreamed of David: his brown hair falling in his eyes, his broad back, the aviator jacket he'd worn in the winter cold. I remembered lying with him in the bathtub in Hawaii, and cooking dinner with him in the kitchen of his cottage. I remembered the first dinner we'd ever had, at Scotto's, when we'd just talked and talked. I remembered watching him lean forward with his eye pressed to the telescope, searching the sky.

One night after work, my coworkers all seemed to have somewhere to go, and nobody wanted to go out to the Water Mill for a drink, but I couldn't tolerate the idea of going home just yet. I drove around Longwood Falls and considered seeing a movie but decided against it, knowing I wouldn't be able to concentrate. Then, as I circled the town for the second time, something impelled me back to the library, which was now dark and locked for the night. I parked the car in my regular space, let myself in with my key, and stood in the front vestibule by the turnstile, looking around. I always loved the library at night, the dark, gleaming sheen of it, the complete sense of emptiness and peace.

Tonight I went through the turnstile and walked up three flights to the newspaper archives. I switched on one of the timer lights there, and as it ticked quietly I searched among the bound copies of the *Longwood Falls Ledger* until I located the volume that included issues from August 1965. I wasn't sure of the exact date I wanted, and so I went through each issue from that month, turning to the obituaries page until I came upon what I'd been searching for.

There it was, a large obituary, the headline reading, "Maggie Thorpe, Olympic Swimmer, Age 36." David's mother had been exactly my age when she drowned. I started to read the obituary, but then the photograph beside it caught my eye and I felt myself involuntarily take in a hard breath.

It was a picture of the swimmer with her son, David, age six. There they were, mother and son. I brought the newspaper closer to my face in order to see better in the dim light of the archives. In the photograph, David was a small boy with a buzz cut, standing beside his mother at the Point, her arm around him, both of them in bathing suits. He had thin legs but a long, straight torso and arms that were beginning to show the first hint of the definition that was to come. He was smiling shyly, the same smile he still wore now, nearly thirty-five years later, and as he smiled his eyes were in a kind of squint. He looked so breathtakingly young, so untouched by the world. But it wouldn't be long after this picture was snapped that his world would collapse into itself, and he would pick up a pair of binoculars and endlessly search the horizon, and later the sky. I lightly traced a finger along the face of this little boy. He was as hopelessly lost to me now as his mother had been lost to him.

How could people just *disappear?* I wondered. It wasn't only through death that you lost them, as Harper had lost Doe forever, but also through love, and through unforgiveness. The truth was that it wasn't just David who was lost now; he and I were both two lost souls, two separately spinning planets. As I sat in the stillness of the late-night library, looking at a long-ago picture of the man I had fallen in love with, a tear dropped lightly down onto the ancient newsprint, followed a moment later by another. I dried the pages of newspaper lightly with the back of my hand, and just then the timed light in the aisle clicked off, leaving me to silently say good-bye in darkness to the vanishing image of that lost little boy.

I stayed in the archives all night, sitting on the cool tiles of the floor, hugging my knees and crying silently for a long time. I must have fallen asleep there, though I don't really remember. The next thing I knew, a very sweet old janitor who'd worked at the library since I was a little girl was gently shaking me awake. I looked up, shocked, at the man in the green uniform. He stood with a rolling industrial bucket and mop. From the tall windows at the end of the aisle, early-morning light was starting to stream into the room.

"Good morning, Miss Mallory," he said to me with a slight trace of worry in his voice.

"Oh, good morning, George," I said, trying to sound nonchalant. "I must have fallen asleep here last night." I stood and stretched, as though it was a perfectly ordinary thing for the head librarian to be discovered fast asleep and fully dressed in the aisle of her library first thing in the morning.

Then I pushed back through the turnstile and out the front door of the library, stepping into the daylight. But I kept thinking of David's face, imagining him at six years of age and then imagining him now, as a grown man. I knew suddenly and definitively that I had to be with him again. I had to say I was sorry for my part in all this—my abruptness when I left, my refusal to listen to what he had to say, my feelings of inferiority to Harper that had colored everything in my life.

So I got back into my car, bleary-eyed from the night in the library, and went to a gas station to fill up the tank. Then I drove all the way back down to Stone Point without stopping. I'm certain I exceeded the speed limit; all I knew was that I had to see him now, had to tell him that I wanted to return to him for good. As I drove, I felt pleasure coming back to me; it flooded me the way it had when David and I had first fallen in love. *I was going back to him.* I turned on the car radio and sang to an old rock song, imagining one day dancing with David to this same song, feeling our hands touching, our hips lightly colliding, our eyes meeting and silently sending each other messages.

I arrived in Stone Point in the late afternoon and went straight to Red Briar, straight to Stardust. Along the way I passed The Eaves, and I wondered if Harper and Nick were home, and what they were doing.

Maybe they were playing Clue. Though I felt a pang about Nick, and a strong desire to see him as well, I knew I wouldn't try to repair that rift during this visit to Stone Point. This visit was for David only.

I drove my car slowly up the path of Red Briar, feeling so relieved to be back here that at one point I had to stop the car for a moment and compose myself. The trees were fully in bloom now, and everything looked fertile and gorgeous. If David would have me back, I'd soon be living here, as we'd planned, walking along this path with him under the arching trees. Where were the red briars? I realized I'd never asked him that. There was a great deal of property that I'd never seen, and we would have time to explore it thoroughly together. *If* he would have me, I reminded myself, for I couldn't be sure he'd still want me back.

As I approached the observatory, I noticed that David's car wasn't there. He was out; this was disappointing, but I would wait. I parked and walked up to the cottage, deciding to peer though the windows and look inside at that place I loved. But the shades were drawn in the middle of the afternoon. I quickly walked to the front door and knocked. There was no answer, and then I remembered something.

I reached into my pocket for my key ring. There, nestled among my house and car and library keys, was the gold key that David had given me, and that I had never used. Carefully I separated it from the others and inserted it into the lock on David's door. Then I turned the knob, and the door gently swung open. I walked inside, and stood in the middle of his living room, feeling a shock that I almost can't begin to describe.

All of the furniture was gone. All of his things were gone. The entire room was empty, the floor covered with a light layer of dust. Real dust, not stardust. I'm not sure how long I stood there, staring and staring.

But the next thing I knew, I heard a man's voice behind me.

"David?" I said instinctively, quickly turning around.

Before me stood a stranger. He was elderly and wearing a pair of overalls. He hoisted a pair of hedge clippers over one shoulder. "Can I help you, miss?" he asked.

"What happened to David?" I said in a controlled but frantic voice. "David Fields?"

"Well," said the man, scratching his chin with an earth-dusted hand. "I'm just the gardener, you understand, but if you're talking about the gentleman who lived here in the cottage . . ." He took a breath, trying to remember details.

"Yes, l am," I said. "Do you know where he is?"

"He's moved away," the gardener went on. "Can't say where exactly. Mr. Boyd said something about Europe, I think, and told me I could use the cottage for storage of my gardening equipment, at least for a while. Mr. Boyd said he might rent the place to someone else—a young couple up from Texas. Newlyweds. This'll be their honeymoon cottage, I guess. A great place for a young couple, don't you think? Kind of romantic, in its own way."

I sank down to the floor, sitting there for a moment in a daze. I didn't know what to do, what to think. I thought I might get sick.

"Are you all right, miss?" the gardener asked me, but I couldn't speak. I shook my head, stood up slowly, and then hurried out of the cottage.

Months went by, and I never told anyone that I had gone back to Stone Point that day. I kept it all to myself: my new wave of sorrow, my resignation that David was really gone for good. And as I continued to live inside all that sorrow and resignation, something else started to stir in me, too. It was a kind of restlessness, I think. Summer in Longwood Falls had turned to fall, and there was once again a snap in the air, which reminded me that winter was coming soon, and that it was only a little while before I'd feel my aloneness with an intensity that always came on in Longwood Falls when the weather grew cold and people retreated to their separate homes.

I thought I might shrivel up and disappear if I was alone again for another winter. And so I did something I'd never imagined I would do: I finally let Jeff Hardesty take me to dinner.

He'd stopped at the library several times since he first moved back, and we'd had short, pleasant enough chats, keeping each other up-to-date on our lives. In Buffalo he'd briefly been married to another lawyer, and their subsequent divorce was straightforward and amicable. They hadn't had children. When he asked me about my own life, I was vague, talking about work first and then, when pressed, giving him a short, abridged version of my time in Stone Point, and the story of David. Now, one day in late November, nine months since I'd seen David, something in my smile must have given Jeff encouragement when he stopped into the library on his lunch break. David was living somewhere in Europe, perhaps already in love with another woman. David was off seeing the world, while I was still here, in the place where I'd always been. I had to find a way to get over him; I couldn't spend the rest of my life thinking only of the man I'd once loved and lost. So I agreed to have dinner with the man I'd once been involved with but hadn't loved. And apparently hadn't lost.

At the end of that evening with Jeff, which went smoothly and uneventfully, he asked if he could see me again. I gazed at this unexciting but decent man who stood there in a slightly creased dark brown suit and tie, this man I had known years earlier, but in some ways hardly remembered. I compared this with how I'd felt at the end of my first date with David. My entire body had been awakened that night in Stone Point, snapped to attention as if through some hidden source of electricity. But now I just felt pleasantly tired. I told Jeff sure, it would be fine to get together again soon. But I didn't give him any indication that I would be excited if he were to call me. Still, he didn't seem to mind.

"Why did we break up, anyway?" he asked me as we stood on my front porch under the yellow light. Moths circled overhead.

"I'm not sure exactly why," I said, although that wasn't really true. We had broken up because neither of us was in love with the other. Surely he must have remembered that. But it seemed as though he didn't, or as though, if he did, he didn't care. Maybe Jeff's definition of love had changed over time, opening up to include not only what was deeply and stirringly felt, but also what was simply comfortable.

I went out with Jeff Hardesty again, and then again after that. On weekends we had an unspoken agreement to see each other, usually on Saturday night, the way we used to do. We'd have dinner at a local restaurant and then go to a movie, or occasionally we'd have dinner at my house or Jeff's, and then watch a video. We'd always choose the video together, standing side by side in Longwood Falls's only video store, combing the racks for something that would appeal to both of us. Standing in a video store on a Saturday evening was a very couplelike thing to do. All around us were other couples doing the same exact thing: teenagers in love, and young marrieds in their twenties, and long-marrieds with wedding rings and a casual ease together.

Jeff and I could easily become like them, a man and a woman of a certain age who have decided to spend their lives together. A man and a woman on a Saturday night, looking for something to fill the space between them. We'd take the video home with us, and after dinner we'd settle in on the couch, and watch. Sometimes, if we were at my house, Jeff would fall asleep on the couch after the movie, and I would cover him with an afghan and let him spend the night there.

One night, after he'd been asleep for a

while on the couch and I'd gone upstairs to bed, I woke up to hear someone saying my name. I looked up in the dim room and saw Jeff standing by my bed. "Can I join you?" he whispered in the darkness. "It's been so long, Liz."

I looked at him. Jeff was devoted to me, and would never hurt me the way David had. So he wasn't exciting, so he didn't have the passion and sadness and depth that David had; what good had those qualities done me, anyway?

I nodded, not saying a word, and Jeff slipped into the bed beside me, as he used to do. He smelled of sleep, and, oddly, of a closet full of linens. It was a safe smell, familiar, homelike, not thrilling but somehow reassuring. He was a good man, I reminded myself as he gently looped his arms around me and began to kiss my face, my neck, my hair.

"Liz," he whispered to me. "You don't know how much I've wanted this. Ever since I moved away, I've thought about you."

Did it matter that I hadn't thought of him, too? Did it matter that he cared about me more than I did about him? I told myself that we could manage, that it was rare for affections to be equal, to be reciprocal, the way they had seemed for a while between David and me.

In the morning, I woke up to find Jeff's arm thrown across me. When he opened his eyes and realized where he was, his face brightened into an easy smile that made me see how happy he was that we were back together. But for me, happiness was an elusive thing. I knew that I couldn't find it here, on this bright morning, the sun pouring into the bedroom where I lay with a kind, easy-going lawyer who asked so little of me. But I also knew that, having found it once before in my life, I wasn't likely to find it again. And so I put my arms around him and we sank deeper into the bed.

As the weeks passed, Jeff and I once again became known in Longwood Falls as a couple. We were invited to dinner parties together, and we even jointly subscribed to a season of theater in Albany, about an hour away. My friends said they were very happy for me, and they loved the story of our reunion. It was funny the way people could be happy for you when you weren't necessarily all that happy yourself. But even though my feelings about Jeff could never go past a certain point, I enjoyed the idea that people assumed I was perfectly content. I told myself that the illusion of contentedness might someday magically transform into the real thing.

One night, after Jeff and I had just finished a quiet supper together at my house and were settling down in front of the VCR for an old Katharine Hepburn movie we'd rented, he suddenly took my hands in his. I noticed the intensity of his expression, and was taken aback. The opening credits of the movie were rolling, but he had something he needed to say.

"Liz, listen to me," he said. "I've told you

how glad I am that things are going so well between us. But I also see that you're cautious. And you have a right to be. We tried to make this work once before." He took a breath; this was clearly hard for him. "You haven't talked about it much, but I know that you're still getting over that man you were involved with. Daniel, wasn't that his name?"

"David," I said softly.

"David, right," said Jeff. "And I guess I'm just hoping," he went on, "that maybe one day you'll get over him completely, and start to feel really good about you and me. That you'll feel I'm right for you."

"Jeff," I said, "you're a very nice man."

"I don't want to be a 'nice man,' " he said quickly. "That's not something anyone wants to be. I mean, it's fine to be nice, but I want to be more than that. I want you to be glad to see me at the end of the day, and glad to see me when you wake up in the morning. I want to be married to you eventually, to spend our lives together. Do you think that's even remotely possible?"

I looked at him. Did I think it was possible? Anything was, I thought. "Yes," I said in a soft, flat voice.

"Well, that's great," he said.

At that moment, I happened to notice that the moon looked particularly luminous tonight, that it was pouring its reflected light into the window of my living room. It was a full moon, and the shadows and crevices and etching of imperfections could be seen even from this great distance. The moon was amazing, I thought, looking up at it in wonder, this moon that shone down on Jeff and me. This moon that shone down on David, somewhere on another continent. If David were here right now he would have stood and stared at the moon; we would have stood and stared at it together for a long time, not saying a word.

"Look at that moon," I told Jeff, and he obediently turned and looked.

"What about it?" he asked, slightly puzzled.

"What *about* it?"

"Yes," he said.

"Well, isn't it beautiful?" I asked.

He took a moment. "Looks like a moon to me, Liz," he said, shrugging. Then he said, "Is there something here that I'm missing? I mean, is it a special moon or something? Some sort of unusual moon?"

I shook my head. "No," I finally said in a very quiet voice. "It's not special. Forget it."

He turned away from the window, back to the television. "Come on," he said. "Enough about the moon. The movie's starting."

Then we sat back and watched our movie, his hand in mine.

Chapter
Nine

∞ More than a year had passed since my stay in Stone Point, a long parade of months that were less lonely than I was accustomed to, yet somehow more unsettling. I wasn't alone anymore; I had a steady relationship with someone who cared about me. But still I felt uncomfortable with the way I'd accepted Jeff into my life when in fact I still didn't feel a great deal for him. Ours was a partnership that everyone I knew heartily approved of, a journey of two people who had been lonely for a long time, and now supposedly weren't lonely anymore.

But when I sat with Jeff in restaurants or at the theater, or when I waited for him to pick me up at the library after work, I felt lonelier than I'd ever been, and I tried hard to imagine that it was David I was with, or David I was waiting for. But David, of course, was long gone.

When Jeff and I had been together for six months, he decided we should celebrate the anniversary by having drinks at the Water Mill. I didn't particularly feel like celebrating, but it seemed important to him, so we sat at a rickety table in the back of the bar that night and toasted each other with glasses of champagne.

"To a great half-year," Jeff said as we held up our glasses. Then he added, "I'm so glad to have you back."

Our glasses lightly chimed together, and the sound seemed to me like a bell that signified the beginning of the rest of my life. Suddenly I felt dizzy and strange, and I put down my glass without taking the requisite sip. My hand shook, and some of the champagne sloshed over the rim. I realized that I felt like bursting into tears.

"Are you okay, Liz?" Jeff asked, and when

I didn't answer he leaned forward, taking my hand.

I knew, at that moment, that I couldn't continue seeing him anymore; it wasn't fair. So I told him, speaking slowly and carefully and apologizing over and over again.

After his initial astonishment, he said, "I thought we had something good here." He put down his own glass.

"We did, Jeff," I said. "But do you really think 'good' is enough? This is what we went through last time, isn't it? Except last time, you agreed with me. But now you don't seem to."

"I don't know what's enough," he said in a hard voice. "I just know that we'd found something nice together. And that this time it was a relief. Neither of us is getting any younger, in case you hadn't noticed."

I tried to tell him I was sorry again, and to make him see that what he felt for me he would certainly feel for someone else. But he said he didn't want to talk about it anymore, and he reached into his wallet, extracted some bills, and left them on the table. Then he said he had to go, and he turned and left me sitting in the back of the bar with a full glass of champagne fizzing and settling in front of me.

For a long time, I felt terrible about Jeff. When we passed each other in town we nodded hello but didn't stop to speak. One day, I saw him in the window of a restaurant with another woman, a paralegal at his firm who had long dark hair and a pretty smile. They were sharing a big plate of fried zucchini and laughing; I hoped they were happy.

My thoughts turned inevitably back to David, as they always seemed to. I often summoned David up in my thoughts, and sometimes images of Harper and Nick came to mind, too. Aunt Leatrice kept me up-to-date about my sister and my nephew as best she could, but it wasn't the same as actually being in touch with them. It seemed to me as though Stone Point, and everyone associated with the place, was part of a dream I'd once had a long time ago. Had I really lived at The Eaves, and fallen in love with a man named David Fields beneath the dome of an observatory? Yes, I had, but none of it mattered anymore; none of it had any relevance to my life in Longwood Falls.

Then one Saturday afternoon in September, a clear, vivid autumn day, I came home from a trip to the grocery store to find a car in my driveway. It was a sleek black Town Car, and just then the back door opened and Harper stepped out. I was so startled that my groceries almost slipped from my arms.

It had been eighteen months since I had seen her, and the change in her appearance was startling. Her hair was longer, about the same length as mine, and her face looked full, flushed, livelier than it had. She wore a cornflower blue dress, a blazer, and a simple strand of onyx beads.

"Harper," I said, trying to keep my voice calm, "what are you doing here?"

"I came to bring you an invitation," she

said. She reached into a pocket of her blazer and pulled out an envelope. As I unfolded the piece of stationery inside, I could see her maroon monogram embossed on the cream-colored bond paper.

PLEASE COME TO AN OPENING

OF AN EXHIBIT OF

HARPER MALLORY'S RECENT WORKS.

SUNDAY, SEPTEMBER 18TH, 4 P.M.,

AT THE PAINTER'S STUDIO AT THE EAVES,

STONE POINT, NEW YORK.

"But that's tomorrow," I said, confused. "I can't possibly just leave everything and—"

"Please," said my sister. "Please try."

"It's an awfully long way to come just to hand me an invitation," I said.

"I really want you there, Liz. I can't tell you how much," said Harper. I didn't respond. We stood there for a moment, and finally Harper said, "I've been in this car for hours. And so has my driver. Are you at least going to offer us something cold to drink?"

I nodded, going first to say hello to the driver, who I'd met before, and who said he didn't need a drink, and that he'd prefer to stay in the car. Then I opened the front door of my house, letting Harper inside, and for the first time in many years she entered the place where we'd grown up together.

She stood for a while looking around in a kind of wonder. "All this time," she said, "I've remembered the house as being so small, so ordinary. But it's nice here, Liz, it really is. You made it nice."

We walked into the kitchen and I began putting away my groceries. "I did what I could," I told her. "It's not much."

"No, you really put your heart into it," she said softly, and I knew that this was true. For years I'd put my heart into my house and my job at the library, instead of into another person.

When everything was put away, Harper and I went and sat on the sunporch, which was slightly cold but streaming with light, and I poured her a mug of fresh cider. She settled herself in, taking a few long sips and leaning back against the cushioned chair before beginning to speak.

"You know, there are some things about what happened that you don't understand," she finally said. I waited for her to go on, not knowing what she was getting at. "I never got a chance to tell you why I broke things off with David," she continued.

"You told me you were on the rebound from your marriage," I said.

"I was," she said. "But that wasn't all. I also stopped seeing him . . . because he was wonderful."

I looked at her. "That doesn't make any sense."

"Not to you, maybe," she said. "But to me it does. The thing is, I felt that I didn't deserve someone like David. Someone kind and thoughtful. Someone who actually listens. I already told you that when I first met him, my interest in him was purely based on physical attraction, nothing more than that."

"I don't think I need to hear about this," I tried to interrupt.

But Harper wouldn't quit. "Yes, you do," she said. "The thing is, as we kept seeing each other, I started to find out what he was really like, how special he was, and it scared me."

"Why?" I asked, not comprehending.

"I have a bad track record with men," said Harper. "As you may have noticed." I saw that she looked on the verge of tears, and I didn't understand the reason for her sudden display of emotion. "You're the good one, Liz, not me," she said. "The entire time we were growing up, I always had to hear from Mom and Dad and Aunt Leatrice and all the teachers in school and practically everyone we knew about how thoughtful and responsible you were. How kind and courteous and everything. You were the *good* twin. Which made me, by default, the bad one." She took a breath, then said, "So I guess I never felt that I deserved a good man."

I was stunned. "I had no idea that you ever gave me a second thought, Harper," I said quietly.

"Oh, you were always on my mind, Liz," she said. "I knew I'd never be able to stop comparing us."

"I thought that was *my* job," I said.

"It worked both ways," she replied. "I had to get away from Longwood Falls. In high school, you were so smart and focused and responsible. I knew I couldn't live up to that, and I didn't want to try. Mom and Dad were clearly disappointed that I was so different."

"They weren't disappointed in you," I said. "They were disappointed in me! They were proud of you, Harper; I know that for a fact." But in that moment I saw that there were two sides to every story, even a story about growing up. Neither of us knew the truth, because there wasn't one singular truth; there were many.

She put down her mug of cider. "And *I* know for a fact," she said, "that David wasn't happy with me when we were involved."

"Come on, he was obsessed with you," I said. "He said that when you left him he was just devastated."

But Harper shook her head. "I think, if he were to really face what happened, he'd see that he was relieved when I broke up with him. Oh, he was devastated all right that he'd been *left*. Because of his mother, in some way he felt as though that was happening all over again. But he would have felt devastated being left by *any* woman, not just me." She shook her head. "He and I were totally wrong for each other, and he knew it. Everything about us was different. Yes, I suppose he's a simpler person than I am, but I don't mean that as an insult. I just mean that he doesn't require too much to get him through life." She smiled ruefully. "Me, I'm high maintenance," she said. "And I always will be."

I couldn't help but nod in agreement. We sat there in silence for a while; it was taking me quite some time to absorb everything she'd just said. I'd had no idea Harper had grown up feeling a certain kind of inferiority to me, nor had I known the actual reason that she had broken up with David. But as much as I was shocked by what she'd just told me about the breakup, I knew it didn't matter anymore. All of this was in the past.

What did matter, I thought, was whether or not I could forgive her, whether she and I could move beyond what had happened and stay in each other's lives. I realized, as I sat with her, that I was beginning to feel a sensation of contentment, the kind that comes when you're with someone you've known forever. And Harper and I had literally known each other forever. We'd known each other since before forever had even begun.

"About that art show of yours," I said quietly. "I'm not sure I have anything to wear."

"You'll really come?" she asked, and I nodded.

It bothered me, of course, that Harper would arrive the day before the show and assume I'd simply be able to drop everything and return to Stone Point with her. It bothered me that she was right. I was the good twin, after all, and so I agreed that I would drive back to Stone Point with her that evening so that I could attend her art show the next day. Besides, I was excited at the idea of seeing Nick, and of trying to find a way to get him to forgive me. And if Harper and I were ever going to make our peace, then I would have to return to Stone Point eventually, anyway; I would have to purge that town of its significance, of its inevitable former connection to David. So, I decided, I might as well start now.

As I went upstairs to pack my weekend bag for the trip, Harper wandered around the house, looking through the rooms that made up her own past. After a moment I heard her exclaim. "Oh my God, Liz," she called. "Look at this."

I came downstairs and went to the pantry, where she was standing and pointing to the inside of the door. There on the wall, faint but still visible, were the pencil marks our mother had made to measure our heights over the years. *H*, she had written next to a mark, and then *L*, and then the date. Here was our childhood, and here was our adolescence, written on a pantry door in soft graphite, so many years ago. Time was dazzling to me; where had it gone? How had we gotten from *there* to *here*? We weren't those girls anymore, those two girls who wanted nothing to do with each other, those two Mallory girls who grew further and further apart with every inch.

Now Harper grabbed a pencil. "Stand here," she intructed me, and I stood obediently with my head touching the door, and she made a new mark, higher than all the others, which I stepped back to regard. Then she handed the pencil to me and stood where I'd been standing. I wrote a tiny line on the wall by the top of her head, and then I added the date. As always, the lines were at the same level. Then, in a moment of quiet intensity, we both stood back to look at the pantry door, marveling at how we'd grown.

*   *   *

Later, sitting together in the backseat of her Town Car for six hours, my sister and I talked about everything we'd never really gotten around to talking about over the course of our lives. We went over old history, discussing various people we'd grown up with, and teachers we'd had, and what had become of them. We reminisced about our parents, about the way our father used to sing "Good Night, Irene" when he was putting us to bed, and how deep and resonant his voice had been.

We talked about our various disappointments in life, and the moments of triumph we'd experienced. We were careful not to talk about David anymore. Instead, we laughed and stirred up old, safe memories, and I knew how much pleasure Aunt Leatrice would have had to see us together like this. At one point during the trip, when the mood had grown serious and quiet, Harper began to talk to me about Doe, about how much she missed her, and what she had been like.

"In many ways she was a miniature version of me, but in other ways she was nothing like me," she said. "She could be very remote like Carlo. It's always two people who make a child. No child comes out exactly like one parent or the other. But I didn't really know that, and in a way, after the divorce, it was as though Doe was mine." She paused. "Which meant that Nick was Carlo's, except Carlo wasn't around. So Nick was on his own. I feel very bad about that now. I've been trying to make it up to him; I think it's going to take a long time."

"How is Nick doing?" I asked.

"He's okay," she said. "He's struggling along, like any nine-year-old boy who thinks he has to be the man of the house."

Nine. Had he really gotten that old?

"You were a wonderful influence on him," Harper said. "He loves to read by himself now, did you know that? He spends a lot of time in his room late at night, his head buried in a book. He's doing pretty well, I think." She paused. "It's been over a year and a half since Doe's accident," she said. "And I guess it's almost been that long since he's seen you."

"Will he ever forgive me?" I asked.

"Life is long," said Harper. "Sometimes." There was a pointed silence. She reached into her purse, scrabbling around inside for a moment, and I assumed she was going to take out a cigarette, which she often did when she was upset. Instead she took out a hard candy, which she unwrapped and put into her mouth.

"No cigarette?" I asked.

"I was wondering when you'd notice," Harper said. "I quit seven months ago. Nick insisted."

"Good for him," I said.

"He came up to me one day with this serious expression on his face, and he told me that he'd already lost a sister, and that he barely had a father, and that he didn't want to lose me as well." Her voice was shaky with emotion. "That was the last time I ever smoked. I just threw them away. It's been tough," she went on, "but I had to do it. He needs me badly."

"Yes," I said. We rode in silence. Then, after a moment, I said, "Harper, tell me. What do *you* need badly?"

"Me?" she said. "Well, I know this seems hard to believe, because I know I said I'm high maintenance, but actually, when it comes right down to it—at least emotionally—I need very little." She looked out the window at the trees rushing past.

"But do you think you'll want to fall in love again someday?" I persisted. "Do you think you'll ever want to settle down with someone? Someone *good?*"

My sister smiled wearily. "Maybe someday," she said. "But I can't even begin to think about it for a long, long time. For me, this time in my life isn't about falling in love. It's about remembering Doe. My little girl."

Her voice broke, and she put her hands to her face and held them there for a moment. I didn't move closer to her, because I suspected she wouldn't want me to. Harper was used to moments like this, and there would be more of them.

I imagined my sister heading down the road in Stone Point toward the hill where Doe was killed. That hill would be covered with a veil of skittering leaves now, and children were probably rolling in those leaves every day. Everything had changed since I'd come to Stone Point a year and a half ago. Snow had melted, then returned, then melted again. Leaves had fallen. Entire lives had opened up in that town and been transformed. I'd changed, too, but then I'd changed back again. I was still the head librarian in Longwood Falls, still locked into the life I'd led there for so many years. But maybe I hadn't really changed back; it almost never worked that neatly. David had changed me forever, I knew, and because of it, I was a different person now.

When we arrived in Stone Point, night had fallen. Tom and Jeannette welcomed me back into The Eaves. The household wasn't as formal and reserved as it had once been.

Instead, it seemed to be a different sort of place: a household that was finally showing signs of being a home.

"Can I go upstairs and find Nick?" I asked, and Harper said of course. I walked faster and faster, practically breaking into a run as I headed toward his room. The door was open, and he was sitting in the lower bunk of his bunk bed and reading a novel, one of those paperback books with blood and slime on the cover. I approached him carefully, the way I'd done the first day I'd arrived. "Hi, Nick," I said.

He looked up, shocked to see me, and then he quickly sprang to his feet. "Aunt *Liz*?" he said, and in that moment I was shocked, too. He was so much longer and lankier now. He almost looked like a different person. His face had taken on a real maturity, and I could almost get a sense of how he would look when he was grown, how handsome he would be, like his father. On his wall were taped some posters of race cars and basketball players, replacing the framed prints of jungle scenes that used to be there. And then I noticed, on the top of the dresser next to his bed, a small object: the piece of volcanic rock that he'd begged me to bring back from Hawaii.

"What are you doing here?" Nick asked me. He'd recovered from his shock at seeing me and seemed to remember that he was very angry with me.

"Your mother brought me," I said. "To come see her art show."

"Oh, so you're not staying," he said.

"No. I have a life up in Longwood Falls," I said. "A job. A house. I know it's easy to forget that." I paused, and then I added, "Back when I was staying here, I almost forgot it myself."

"Well, I should keep on with my reading," said Nick, and he turned away from me.

"Oh, for God's sake," I said, exasperated, "please stop this right this minute."

He turned back to me and regarded me for a long moment. "You left me, Aunt Liz," he said. "I thought we were friends."

"We are," I said. "And we always will be. I'm very sorry I let you down, Nick, that I left in such a hurry. I guess it didn't give you time to mourn, did it?" I saw his expression shift slightly, almost flinching. "It's like with Doe," I added softly. "First she was here, and then she wasn't. I did that, too, and I wasn't fair to you."

He tried to look away from me because he knew he appeared upset, and he was embarrassed. "I guess not," he said.

"Nick, I didn't think it through at the time, and I'm very ashamed of myself," I said. "Please don't hold this against me forever. It was a long time ago, a year and a half. Please be my favorite nephew again."

"I'm your *only* nephew, Aunt Liz," he reminded me.

"Well, that's true," I said. "But you know what I mean. Can't we be the way we were? Can't we play endless games of Monopoly and Clue?"

"I don't play those games anymore, Aunt

Liz," he said in a scornful voice. "I put them away in the basement. I'm into chess now."

"Well, did you know I'm a real whiz at chess?" I tried. "A grand master, in fact."

He looked at me skeptically. "You are not," he said.

"I guess you'll have to find out for yourself," I told him, and at this point he broke into the slightest of smiles. "Oh, come here, Nick," I said, and I moved toward him and gathered him to me. Despite himself, he came willingly, as if relieved to be forced not to be mad at me anymore.

Harper, Nick, and I spent the next morning taking a long walk around the grounds of the estate, and I marveled at the way the property looked in autumn, colorful and burnished in gold and bronze and copper. My sister and I continued the conversations we'd begun in the car; we had so much talking to make up for, and it seemed as though we'd never run out of things to say.

∽

In the afternoon, we headed to the studio shortly before four o'clock, when the other guests for the art show were scheduled to arrive. "Come on in," Harper said, opening the unlocked door. "I wanted you to be the first to see it."

I walked in tentatively; the last time I had been here had been so traumatic, and now I had no idea of what I'd find. Today, the beautiful white room was filled with paintings I'd never seen before. They looked different from any of Harper's previous work. They weren't tormented or dreamlike, and their subjects weren't people; instead, these were pictures of various animals and objects and places. And they were all exquisite.

At first, I didn't understand the significance of the work, but simply admired it as I walked around the large room. There was a painting of a horse, its neck dipped down to graze in a field, and another painting of an ice cream stand at twilight, a neon cone illuminating the sky. There was a picture of a sailboat, and another one of a child's ballerina costume hanging in a closet. Then, suddenly, I came upon a painting of an old doll with a tattered red-checked dress. I stopped in front of it, realizing, with a start, that it was a picture of the doll I'd given Doe when she was just born.

At her funeral, her friend Caitlin had stood up and told everyone that Doe had recently given the doll to her in friendship, because it was something that Doe had always loved. I realized now that Harper's art show was made up of paintings of *all* the things that Doe had loved. The show was a celebration of Doe, not a maudlin tribute to a child who had died, but one that was filled with the things that had once excited and engaged that child, and filled her with life.

I turned to my sister. "Oh, Harper," I said. "You've really done it."

Then I embraced her, and both of us began to cry. We cried for Doe, who had graced Harper's life for eight short years, and who had then left her forever. Harper would never see that beautiful little girl again, no matter how hard she looked.

"I still have that dream," she said. "The unbearable one in which you see the person who's died—in this case, Doe—and she tells you, 'Mommy, I didn't die after all,' and you're so happy you can hardly believe it. You start kissing her and hugging her, and you're ecstatic." Harper took a breath. "And then you wake up," she said. "And you find out it was only a dream. She isn't alive after all, and she never will be." She shook her head sadly. "But it's not just dreams," she said. "It's daydreams, too. I think about what Doe would have been like as she got older. I picture her at seventeen, with long red hair, and maybe a tattoo, even a nose ring or something, sprawled out across her bed endlessly talking on the telephone to her friends. And me having to tell her to get off. And I picture her later on, going out into the world on her own. Taking her to college, helping her set up her room." She paused. "I even picture her getting married, can you believe it?" She wiped at her eyes as she spoke, but the tears kept coming. She ignored them and just continued talking. "I like to think she would have met someone who would have cherished her," she said.

"Oh, she would have, Harper," I said.

"Someone who would have loved her so much, and who would have taken care of her as they went through life together," Harper went on. She took a ragged breath. "When you're a parent, you're always having to let go," she said. "It happens in little ways all the time, and it's the hardest thing in the world. But I guess if you let it happen the way it's supposed to, then someday that little girl will grow up and fall wildly in love with some wonderful man. And maybe you can see that she'll still be taken care of, that they'll both take care of each other as long as they live."

After she finished talking, Harper and I cried and cried. We cried loudly and openly and freely, in a way we never had. It felt very good to cry like that with her, and I remembered that my sister's ex-husband, Carlo, had wanted me to make sure that Harper would have someone she could talk with, someone she could cry with. Well, she had someone now, I thought as I held her in the middle of the studio, not wanting to let go.

Afterward, we sat together on the floor of that room for quite a while, drinking glasses of white wine that Harper poured for us, and eating stoned-wheat crackers and slivers of gouda cheese.

"You were never going to paint again, remember?" I said. "You made a pronouncement about it."

Harper nodded. "I believed it at the time," she said. "I didn't understand that painting was the only thing that would save me. But it did, Liz; it kept my hands busy and it distracted me. And then, finally, it helped me face things head-on. But it took a long time. It's still an ongoing process, actually. I think it always will be."

We talked for a while longer. I glanced at

my watch a few times, for it was after four-thirty, and no one else had arrived.

"When are the other people coming?" I asked her. "Didn't the invitation say four o'-clock?"

Harper smiled. "I have a confession. There are no other people."

I was puzzled. "But isn't this an art show?"

She nodded. "Yes," she said. "But I only invited one person. You." She paused. "I really wanted to see you, and I knew Nick did, too, secretly, even though he wouldn't admit it. And I wanted you to see my work. It was the only way I knew how to get you here." Suddenly she stood up. "Actually, there's one more painting I want you to see," she said. "It's not part of this series."

"It's nothing that will upset me, is it?" I asked.

Harper smiled slightly. "No," she said.

I followed her to an easel facing the far wall. In one swift motion Harper turned the easel around on its delicate legs.

Facing me was a picture of a woman. She looked intelligent, sexually knowing, filled with secrets. Her hair was red, and she held herself with a certain kind of powerful grace. "You made a self-portrait," I said. "It's wonderful."

But Harper shook her head. "No," she said quietly. "This is a portrait of you. It's the way you looked after you met David."

I stared at the painting. I could have sworn it was supposed to have been my sister, but she was saying no. Had I really seemed so different after I met David? Had I really seemed as self-possessed as the picture would suggest? I suppose that I had, but still it was shocking to see hard evidence of this. For what the picture showed was something very simple and ordinary, yet extraordinary, too: a woman in love.

I felt my legs suddenly give way, and I sank down to the floor of the studio as though the breath had been knocked out of me. Harper immediately came and sat beside me.

"Are you all right, Liz?" she asked.

I nodded weakly. "It just threw me for a loop," I said, "that's all. Thinking about how I was with him."

She studied my face. "I didn't know it would affect you like this," she said. "Back at your house you told me you were totally over David."

I waited a long moment, and then I said, "That couldn't be further from the truth." I looked away from her, embarrassed that she was seeing the intensity of my feelings. "But it's so pathetic, isn't it?" I went on. "I mean, here I am, thirty-eight years old and still in love with a man who lives somewhere in Europe."

"Is that what you think?" she asked.

I nodded. "I drove here to see David last year," I said, and I told her how I'd found the observatory cottage empty, and had been informed that David had moved to Europe. "He's probably already married to someone else. He probably has a child already," I said. "He's probably already forgotten me."

"But Liz," said Harper in a soft voice, "he's back."

I stared at her. "Don't make jokes," I said.

"It's not a joke," she said. "He was gone for a year; he went on a sabbatical. I think he put his furniture in storage, so the cottage could be rented for the year. He came back a few weeks ago, in time for the start of school."

My heart was thudding. Harper slid closer to me on the floor and took my hands in hers. "Listen to me," she said quietly. "You can go back to him. It's not too late."

"No," I said. "It is."

"It never is," said Harper.

"I'm sure he's gotten over me," I said. "What we had was amazing, but it was also extremely brief."

"David," said Harper, "takes a long time to get over things. Haven't you noticed?"

That night, after the sky had grown dark, and Harper and Nick had sat down in the family room to play chess, I slipped out of the house and borrowed one of Harper's cars. I drove nervously over the local roads until I came to Red Briar. As I went through the tall iron gates of the estate and past the main house, I could see the top of the observatory's dome poking up above a stand of trees, like the forehead of a giant. There it was: Stardust. And this time, the lights were on.

I drove up to the building, parked Harper's car beside it, and got out. I was apprehensive and shaky, and I felt unprepared to see him. I didn't have a clue as to what I would even say.

Something made me turn then; it wasn't a sound, but was more a sensation of David's presence. He was up on the hill just past the observatory, facing away from me as he had been the first time we'd met, standing there with his telescope. As I walked up the hill, he heard me and turned. Then he just stood and stared, no smile crossing his face, no expression of pleasure or relief or even shock. Just a slow stare, unblinking.

"Are you looking at Saturn?" I heard myself ask.

David shook his head. "No," he said after a moment, and he didn't offer anything more.

I stood several feet away from him, but even from that distance I could see that he looked a little different. He wore his aviator jacket, and his face was slightly darker from the sun. He looked a bit older, handsome but weary, like someone who has been traveling for a long time and was now tired.

"What are you doing here, Liz?" he asked, but his tone of voice made it clear that he wasn't all that invested in the answer.

"I'm not sure," I said.

He fiddled with the screws on his telescope, and peered through the eyepiece at an object far away.

"Is it a star you're looking at?" I asked.

"Actually," he said, "I'm just killing time."

"Oh?"

"There's going to be a meteor shower in a little while," he said flatly. "I won't need the telescope for that."

The Observatory

∞

"A meteor shower?" I said, vaguely remembering such an event from the girls' summer camp I'd attended when I was eight. We were all taken out of our tents late one night to watch the heavens, but I was too tired to appreciate what I saw, and so thirty years later I remembered none of it. "What are meteor showers, exactly?" I asked him.

I saw his face reflexively adopt a teacher's expression. "Once or twice a year," he began, "if we—by 'we' I mean Earth—regularly cross the orbit of a comet, then we'll be hit by this big crowd of meteoroids. Most of the time we can connect the showers with a particular comet. Now, since all the meteors are going along in the same orbit, they'll seem to be coming from the same location in the sky. It's called the 'radiant.' "

"I like that word," I said. " 'Radiant.' It sounds hopeful."

"Things in the sky," he said curtly, "aren't hopeful or unhopeful, or good or bad. They just *are.*" He paused. "That's what I like about them, I guess." He returned to the telescope now, as if his brief, halfhearted interest in me was already faltering.

"You can't even look at me for very long, can you?" I said quietly.

So he did. Hard. He stood and gazed at me defiantly, his arms folded across his chest. "Here. I'm looking at you. But why should I?" he asked. "I put myself out there for you. I begged you to at least talk things through with me. I called you up and left those messages, but you never called back. You acted like what we'd had together didn't matter at all." After this flood of words he stopped talking for a moment, and then, in a quieter voice, he added, "I didn't know you could be so cruel."

I waited a second, then I said, "But you did know. That's the one thing you've always known about the world."

"What do you mean?" he asked.

"You said so yourself," I said. "It's what

you've always seen up there in your observatory: the way everything in the universe just moves along on its own path, not caring about the destruction it's leaving behind. Things freezing, or burning up. The loneliness of the planets." I took a breath. "You were drawn to it because of what happened to you when you were six. I mean, things happen up there that can't be undone. Terrible things." I came closer to him, so close that I could see a small pulse fluttering unevenly in his temple. "But there's a difference between what goes on up there and what goes on down *here*, on earth." I swallowed, feeling my throat tighten. "People can be cruel," I said, "and they can make big mistakes."

"Yes, they can," he said.

"But it's what happens next that counts," I said. He kept looking at me, his expression unchanged. "I'm asking you to forgive me," I told him. "Please, David."

"So why did it take you so long to say this?" he asked.

∞

"I came back last year to say it," I said. "I drove all the way here, and I came to the cottage, and it was empty. The gardener told me you were gone. I can't tell you what it did to me. I just fell apart."

He looked at me, his expression perceptibly softening for the first time, shifting as I watched.

"I went to Europe," he said. "I had a sabbatical coming, and I didn't want to stay here; I couldn't stay here, after what had happened with you. I didn't know what else to do, so I went away for a year, knowing that I'd have to come back at the end of it. I guess the gardener didn't know I'd be back." He shrugged. "I went all over the place like some student traveler, basically trying to lose myself in astronomy. I went to Padua, where Galileo lived. And I went to Greenwich, England, and to Stonehenge. I just went from place to place, taking pictures, taking notes, sleeping in these little hotels, traveling around on this self-guided astronomy tour, but I had such a terrible time. I was so lonely, you have no idea."

And at that moment, something happened. A streak filled the night sky, flaring brightly before vanishing.

"Did you—" he said.

"Yes, yes, I saw it," I said.

The meteor shower was beginning, and we both leaned our heads back and simply looked up, waiting for whatever was next. In a moment we were rewarded with another arc of light, impossibly graceful, heartbreakingly brief.

"Look at that," I said quietly. "And it's just fire and ice."

High above us, frozen chunks of rock were burning up as they hurled through space and time. *Fire*, I thought, remembering how we'd held each other in his bed. Then I thought, *ice*, recalling how we'd both, in our own way, betrayed the other. Love was never one thing or another, yet I hadn't known this before, and now I did.

"Yes," David said. "But it's beautiful while it lasts."

He turned away from the sky to look at me. This time, he looked and looked. Then he stepped forward so we were touching, and I leaned my head against his chest. All I'd wanted for so long was to be with David again, to be held by him and to hold him. What I'd wanted had seemed simple, and yet it had taken me such a long time. But here it was, at last: a man and a woman in the middle of their lives, standing together under a sky filled with light.

Coming in 2001

THE FOUNTAIN

*A Novel
by Emily Grayson*

∞ Two days before Casey Becket's twentieth wedding anniversary, her past came back to haunt her, or, at the very least, astonish her. She wasn't prepared for such a visitation—no one ever is—but instead her thoughts were moving her only in the direction of Saturday, and the anniversary party that was to take place. She was sitting at the kitchen table, the place she could often be found, her feet bare against the cool slate tiles, one foot tapping lightly to the percussive strains of jazz that were wafting from the CD player Michael had installed on a shelf above the spice rack. Before her on the table was a yellow legal pad covered with scrawled writing, all of it instructions she'd written to herself about things that needed to be accomplished before the party. It was while Casey was going over the list and seeing what still needed to be done before Saturday, that she saw a flash of movement out the back window, by the fountain.

Someone was there—one of the men from the party rental company, maybe. He was standing by the fountain, staring down into it, as if studying it for signs of life. By Saturday the fountain would be running again, bursts of water shooting upward, a fine mist falling on all the people who gathered in the yard. But now it was completely dry, still clotted with leaves and blossoms that had dropped from the trees that arched overhead. In recent years, and for no particular reason except perhaps the chaos of daily life, Casey and Michael had let it fall into disrepair. She supposed now that it had become a bit of an eyesore, but not so much that it should be an object of fascination for a stranger. An then the man looked up from the fountain, to the house, to the window where Casey Becket sat at a table, staring back at him.

Casey's hand flew involuntarily to her mouth, as if some primitive part of her had recognized him before she could even realize what, or who, she was seeing. And then there was no mistaking it: Some twenty-odd years after he had disappeared from her life, Will Combray had suddenly walked back into it.

She stood up shakily at the table and silently commanded herself to get a grip. For a "grip," whatever that was, really, was what she needed now more than anything. For a moment she and Will looked at each other through the screened window, neither of them saying a word. It was difficult, in this first, adrenalized moment of shocked recognition, to tell the difference between what she was really seeing and what her memory wanted her to see. But even at this distance, even staring through the screen, Casey could identify one thing that hadn't changed at all over the years: Will's smile. It was an expression that she immediately recognized as his, a slight upturn of one side of the lips, as though he'd recently had a shot of novocaine. A sleepy, slow smile that men might barely notice but that women had always loved.

"Hello, vanilla," he said.

It was a nickname from so long ago, and the sound of it now sent a peculiar sensation unraveling though her. The familiar word, in that familiar voice—it was almost as though no time had passed at all. An in a way, Casey realized, she had always known it would be like this when Will returned. Not *if. When.* For as shocking as it was to look out the back window one morning and see the man she'd loved so long ago suddenly appear, it wasn't really surprising. It was, in a way, inevitable. It was as if she'd known all along that Will would one day come back, and that he would do it in the same way he'd left: unexpectedly.

She walked to the kitchen door and threw it open, stepping out into the yard. "It *is* you," she said, and then the two of them just stood there, staring at each other across the lawn as if in a silent endurance contest, neither of them daring to speak or move any closer. There would be no running, no hugging, no open arms and cascading tears of happiness; this was not the kind of reunion that called for the usual displays of unfettered emotion. Instead, Casey and Will just looked and looked, absorbing what they saw, each appraising the way the other had changed and somehow not changed, the overlay of age upon youth, like layers of paint spread on a canvas.

Will Combray and Casey Becket were now a grown man and woman of forty. The last time they had been together, they were teenagers. Their faces had been narrower then, more defined. Both of them had had long, wild hair back then, too. Will was still unmistakably handsome, if slightly thicker-featured, his sand-colored hair threaded with silver. He had once been an eighteen-year-old in a flannel shirt and jeans and scuffed Frye boots, who had occupied all her thoughts, and here he was now, a forty-year-old man in an expensive-looking white cotton shirt and loosened silk tie, probably well-off and apparently tired. He walked closer then, and she noticed that he had a scar on his chin, something that hadn't been there the last time she'd seen him. He'd had a life without her, a life that included other people, and other places, and even a small scar that cut a raised diagonal across his chin, giving him the slightly raffish appearance of a pirate. A pirate executive, she thought giddily.

As for herself, Casey knew she came across as a delicately pretty woman, someone who still seemed youthful and appealing and slightly arty, though perhaps lacking the concentrated girlish beauty she'd once had. For a moment, she felt as

∞

though she might cry, though whether for the eighteen-year-old Will had once been, or for the eighteen-year-old she'd once been, or simply from the exhaustion of the startling moment, she couldn't say.

"I hope I didn't scare you," Will said. And then, in a quieter voice, he added, "You know, you look exactly the way I imagined."

Casey smiled but didn't answer him. There was something tentative in Will's manner that was unfamiliar to her, even perplexing. Once, he'd been brazen, sure of himself in the way only an eighteen-year-old can be—though, she supposed, it was a brazen act to have come here after all these years, and especially after what he'd done to her.

"I guess you want to come in," Casey said after a moment.

"Yes," he said. "If that's okay."

She nodded, though really she had no idea. *Was* it okay? Maybe it was the worst idea in the world; it was impossible to tell. But Casey had no time to think this through, to be rational about the situation, to try to figure out what it might mean that after all these years Will Combray suddenly wanted to see her again, so instead she simply opened the door and let the first man she had ever loved into her house.

They sat together in the kitchen, drinking ice water from tall blue glasses. The kitchen was a place where Casey Becket often spent a good part of her afternoon, not because her culinary skills were particularly extensive, but simply because it was by far the best room in the house, filled with light and plants and an outsized oval maple table that Michael had built when they were first married. "It's because I want there to be lots of people around it," Michael had said when she'd delicately commented on how incredibly large the table was. "Children, and friends, and family," he'd told her. "The whole nine yards." He'd gotten his wish, for the table was always populated. Long meals had often been spent here, with plenty of food and wine for the adults, and juice and milk poured from plastic jugs for the kids, and music drifting in from the speakers, and everybody was always comfortable.

Somehow, though, she doubted that Michael had ever imagined that Will Combray would one day be sitting at this table. It seemed like a betrayal, in fact, for Casey to have even invited him to sit here. But really, she asked herself, what was wrong with it? They were just a man and a woman sitting together, drinking ice water.

Will swallowed almost an entire glass of water at once, and then asked for a refill, which she stood and got for him. Had he been running? Casey wondered. Had he not drunk anything in days? He had a parched quality to him that was puzzling, though maybe, she thought, it came from nerves. *Nerves.* Casey hadn't ever known that Will Combray possessed them. She was waiting for him to explain himself, to tell her how he had wound up here in Longwood Falls, of all places, so long after he'd gone away for

good. But it seemed as though he was planning to take his time. And of course she
would let him, though some part of her
wanted to yank him by his collar and shake
him, shouting harshly in his face, "What in
God's name do you think you're doing
here?"